THE CAPTAIN'S FORTUNE

THE THIRD BOOK IN THE CAPTAIN TRILOGY

Mel J Wallis

Copyright © Mel J Wallis 2023
This book is sold subject to the condition that it shall not, by way of trade or otherwise, be lent, resold, hired out, or otherwise circulated without the publisher's prior consent in any form of binding or cover other than that in which it is published and without a similar condition including this condition being imposed on the subsequent publisher.
The moral right of Mel J Wallis has been asserted.

This is a work of fiction. Names, characters, businesses, organizations, places, events and incidents either are the product of the author's imagination or are used fictitiously. Any resemblance to actual persons, living or dead, events, or locales is entirely coincidental.

This book is dedicated to my mum with whom I first shared the plotlines of the Captains and the generations of women who live with them in the Captain's house. Sadly she never got to enjoy them in a real book as she is no longer with us.

CONTENTS

ACKNOWLEDGEMENTS i
Chapter One *1*
Chapter Two *3*
Chapter Three *9*
Chapter Four *13*
Chapter Five *17*
Chapter Six *20*
Chapter Seven *24*
Chapter Eight *28*
Chapter Nine *32*
Chapter Ten *36*
Chapter Eleven *40*
Chapter Twelve *44*
Chapter Thirteen *48*
Chapter Fourteen *53*
Chapter Fifteen *57*
Chapter Sixteen *59*
Chapter Seventeen *63*
Chapter Eighteen *68*
Chapter Nineteen *70*
Chapter Twenty *73*
Chapter Twenty-One *76*
Chapter Twenty-Two *80*
Chapter Twenty-Three *85*
Chapter Twenty-Four *88*
Chapter Twenty-Five *91*
Chapter Twenty-Six *94*
Chapter Twenty-Seven *98*
Chapter Twenty-Eight *102*
Chapter Twenty-Nine *105*
Chapter Thirty *108*
Chapter Thirty-One *112*
Chapter Thirty-Two *116*
Chapter Thirty-Three *119*
Chapter Thirty-Four *122*

Chapter Thirty-Five	*125*
Chapter Thirty-Six	*128*
Chapter Thirty-Seven	*131*
Chapter Thirty-Eight	*134*
Chapter Thirty-Nine	*137*
Chapter Forty	*140*
Chapter Forty-One	*143*
Chapter Forty-Two	*146*
Chapter Forty-Three	*149*
Chapter Forty-Four	*153*
Chapter Forty-Five	*157*
Chapter Forty-Six	*160*
Chapter Forty-Seven	*163*
Chapter Forty-Eight	*166*
Chapter Forty-Nine	*169*
Chapter Fifty	*173*
Chapter Fifty-One	*177*
Chapter Fifty-Two	*180*
Chapter Fifty-Three	*184*
Chapter Fifty-Four	*189*
Chapter Fifty-Five	*192*
Chapter Fifty-Six	*196*
Chapter Fifty-Seven	*200*
Chapter Fifty-Eight	*203*
Chapter Fifty-Nine	*207*
Chapter Sixty	*211*
Chapter Sixty-One	*215*
Chapter Sixty-Two	*219*
Chapter Sixty-Three	*223*
Chapter Sixty-Four	*226*
Chapter Sixty-Five	*229*
Chapter Sixty-Six	*232*
Chapter Sixty-Seven	*235*
Chapter Sixty-Eight	*237*
ABOUT THE AUTHOR	240

ACKNOWLEDGEMENTS

I really can't believe that I have finally finished the Captain trilogy. My 'Captains' have been part of my world for several years now and I am extremely fond of them. Like many writers the characters in my books are real to me and I will miss them all.

I need to thank everyone who has supported me while I have been drawn into my fictional world of the Captain's House, Folly and the concluding Fortune. You know who you are, but special mention must go to my family. They have continually put up with my incessant rambling about my plotlines and the ongoing crisis of confidence in my abilities as a writer every single day. My friend, Anne, has kept me focused and provided unwavering support at any time of the day and night! Anne has proofread and edited absolutely *everything* many times over without complaint. Not forgetting Fran, who has proofread for me, given sterling feedback when asked and cakes when they were so desperately needed.

The biggest thank-you needs to go to YOU, my readers, who have this book in your hands and have read the others in the Captain trilogy. YOU are who I write for, and I sincerely hope that you enjoy reading my books as much as I enjoy writing them. For the best feeling in the world is to 'get lost in a book'.

Chapter One

The ivy scrambled wildly over the trees, smothering the branches with its tendrils. The leaves had wrapped themselves around the bare branches so tightly that the branches themselves were hidden. The trees grew in a tightly knit pattern, side by side, their vertical trunks reaching up to the sky leaving the tiniest of spaces in between.

The sky was dark, and the air was damp. The ivy leaves dripped moisture which ran down the limbs of the trees and pooled in the damp earth from which they grew. A grey squirrel scampered up the tree and leapt from trunk to trunk coming to a stop at the edge of the forest and jumping down onto the misshapen branch at the foot of the biggest tree.

The branch quivered from the weight of the squirrel before being still again, as the squirrel set off across the marsh searching for the nuts it had hidden so carefully in the autumn to fill its empty tummy, that had laid forgotten until now.

The branch was set a quiver again by a magpie who alighted at the top to rest awhile, before taking flight once more as the light grew stronger in the impending dawn.

A barely perceptible rustle betrayed the arrival of the next visitor which knocked into the branch and left a clump of its grey fluff on a knobbly protrusion that was all that remained of the youthful stem of the tree that was long since gone. The rabbit watched carefully, before leaving the safety of the forest and running in a zigzag fashion across the water-laden dewy grass to nibble at the tender shoots on the other side of the marshland.

A decisive *thud, thud, thud* belied the arrival of the Captain who crossed the marsh with a purposeful stride.

He came to a halt alongside the misshapen branch and took a knife to it, slicing it from the tree. He held the branch in his hands and then up to his eyes to examine the shape in more detail. He licked his lips and grinned with delight at his find. Then tucking it under his arm, he strode away from the wizen copse of trees and back to the house.

As dawn broke the animals returned to the safety of the forest and the trees appeared to huddle together once more, creating an impenetrable dense space, keeping all that lived there unharmed, but now some of its special magic was elsewhere.

As the daylight grew brighter, a house could be seen across the marsh. Its windows glinting in the darkness from the lamplight within. Its warmth bringing a glow of its own to mix with the rising light of the day. The Captain could be glimpsed in the window, gently sanding the branch that was fresh from the old wizen tree, whittling the wood to make the shape stronger and more perceptible. The head of the beast took shape, and its flared nostrils and horns became lifelike, until the branch itself twisted and turned in the Captain's hands. It took on a life of its own, glowing with rich, warm amber colours.

The Captain's 'dragon' stick remained at his side from that moment on. Some said it was his own figurehead, a talisman of his very own. The carved head of the dragon was his protector, or so they said. The eyes of the beast were reputed to be the most precious rubies, but no one could ever get close enough to see for sure.

Chapter Two

Rose sat at the same window several centuries later, illuminated by modern-day electric light to those who looked in, gazing out across the marsh. The marsh grass was heavy with a morning dew. Its long strands bending with the weight of the water droplets, until a light breeze scattered the dew drops, giving the soil some much needed moisture. The creatures that lived on the edges of the marshland drank from the river that meandered around the house and across the marsh on its way to the sea. The small cluster of trees that stood between the house and the folly, broke the flatness of the marshland that remained between the house and the sea which still stood dark, strong and silent as did the tower of the folly as the dawn broke for another new day.

Rose continued to watch from the window gazing into the distance as the light grew and the shadows faded. Her fingers were wound around a small dainty bone China mug adorned with a delicate pattern of roses, which she used when she sought comfort. It was uncanny that most of her treasured possessions had been found somewhere in the house in which she sat. The house she had inherited from her great aunt. The connections between the past and the present were tangible in this house, within this family and were highly prized by Rose. Her affection for the house was instant and all encompassing, even when the house was forlorn and unloved. The traces of the past were treasured and loved, but occasionally, very occasionally, she was unsure of what she had taken on.

Rose looked out into the distance and mulled over what had happened since she moved in and what had unsettled her in the night. She was familiar with the sensations of the past and how they affected the house. She wasn't bothered by the haunted house label that others attached to her home. She felt that she belonged here with her ghostly Captains and more recently their ladies too.

She could not quiet the sense of unease that was rising within her. The trepidation that was making her tummy jump about and making her feel a bit green around the gills. She was alone last night, as Tom, her boyfriend was away visiting his family for a couple of weeks. She was supposed to be going with him to meet his family but at the last minute she had changed her mind. She couldn't explain why she didn't want to go. She made lots of excuses that weren't really believed, and Tom had left a few days ago under a bit of a cloud. They had not fallen out, were on speaking terms but were just being very civil with each other. Tom was hurt that she wasn't going with him, and Lisa her best friend was mortified when she found out. Lisa had been so excited about house sitting in the infamous Captain's House and was very aggrieved when she was told that it was all off, as Rose had decided not to go after all.

Lisa was arriving in a couple of hours, she didn't cancel her planned time off from work as she was going to spend her time in the house with Rose, albeit not on her own as was the original plan. She was all set for her holiday and the fact that Rose was not going away did not deter her in the slightest. Rose giggled as she was still not sure if Lisa was going to turf her out of her own bed in the 'master' bedroom, as that had been promised to Lisa. She was sure that the next couple of weeks were going to be fun but was not looking forward to telling Tom that Lisa was still coming. The fact that Lisa was still coming, and they were going to have a bit of a 'girlie' holiday just the two of them while he was away, was going to go down like the proverbial lead balloon. She shouldn't let that bother her as he hadn't moved in properly yet. He did spend most of his time at the house with her and should really 'officially' move in, but she hadn't asked him to yet. No rhyme or reason, just indecisiveness really. Rose was renowned for being indecisive amongst her friends. Lisa teased her that she didn't want to share her good fortune and her fabulous house with anyone just yet and she was probably right. She wanted the house to be hers, just hers. Val, her closest neighbour and good friend said that she would end up like her batty old aunt if she wasn't careful, especially when she learnt that Rose was not going away with Tom after all. Her old great aunt from whom she inherited the house was famed locally for not wanting to leave it and being an eccentric recluse. Indeed, it was something of a mystery as it was said that she had never left the village in her lifetime. Not even a visit to London on the train. The same local folk boasted that Rose's eccentric great aunt knew every nook and cranny in the house, village, surrounding countryside and the Kent coastline. She was famed for her local tales and much of her local knowledge was lost when she died. She had definitely left her mark when she was alive, but Rose had yet to find much of a presence of her left in her beloved house. The house that she loved just as much as her old aunt had. Or was there? Rose had not peeked into the box she had found hidden in the roots of the old beech tree that had fallen so dramatically in the spring. It was like saving the last present at Christmas, the thrill of having something to look forward to at a time of her choosing.

The odd feeling was fading, but the sense that something was set to happen was still there simmering underneath it all. Rose watched the daylight grow stronger, disappointed that she had not felt or seen anything of her Captain who usually made his presence felt when she needed him. Did this mean that all was well, or that the Captain had vacated his post? She was undecided and felt vulnerable. The Captain's house without a Captain. How odd! She wondered what Lisa would think of that, and what Lisa would make of the odd tin box she had unearthed. She wanted to try and open the box with Lisa. It was the cause of many an argument with Tom that she kept things from him, and it was true she did. Rose acted on gut feelings, and they were telling her she needed to open that box with her good friend, another female. It was a girl thing she was certain, but couldn't explain why. Tom had offered to prise the box open with his tools, but she couldn't bear the thought of it being damaged by his impulsiveness, so she had snatched it from his hands and hidden it away again. After their heated exchange she had seen him kicking around in the dirt with his feet where she had found the box, searching for any extra clues to its contents, despite her telling him to leave well alone.

Her peace was shattered when Lisa arrived; she had driven down from her flat in London in the battered old Micra car her old great aunt had gifted her just before she passed. It was an old joke between them that Lisa was the unlucky one of the pair of them. Rose inherited a picturesque but dilapidated centuries-old house in the country, which would be worth a fortune if she ever decided to sell it and Lisa, the 'poor relation' of sorts although they were not related, had been given an old car by her great aunt, on its last legs, which didn't even have the potential to become a classic.

It was this car that spluttered its way up the driveway to the old house and puttered to a grinding halt just outside the back door, before it seemed to gasp its last breath with a loud grinding noise and an almighty shudder. Lisa's parking was always abysmal, but this time she had surpassed even her best efforts as the car was parked at a crazy angle from the house. The rear of the car took up most of the space around it, which belittled the size of the car to anyone that had the misfortune to want to pass in another vehicle.

Rose had propped the back door open as the weather was warm and sunny, with a lump of old iron fashioned in the shape of a ship's anchor that she had found in the antique shop in the village. When the car had finally stopped and the ancient wheezing from the old engine fell silent, Mowzer shot in through the door out of the way of the 'monster' that had disturbed his slumber in the sun on the doorstep. All that could be seen of Mowzer was a blur, as the black and white feline of the house scampered up the stairs to continue his repose on the middle of the large bed in the master bedroom. The cat then stretched out on the bed in the dappled sunlight that filtered in through the front windows and proceeded to lick his front paw.

As fast as Mowzer scampered in, Rose rushed out, keen to see her best friend again. She had missed her busy, scatty friend. She had hardly seen Lisa since she moved into the house. Her great aunt's property inheritance had not stayed dilapidated for long. With the help of her new friends in the village and her now best friend, Steve, who just happened to be her builder and property maintenance advisor, so he kept telling her when she referred to him as 'her builder', she was living in the house of her dreams, and she seemed to have triumphed against every challenge life had thrown at her while she was living there.

She didn't wait and hang around being polite, for Lisa to come to her with her suitcase in tow. She wanted to throw her arms around her friend and hold her close. The women were best friends because they were so alike and had been friends ever since their early teenage years. Lisa had exactly the same idea and she almost fell out of the car in her haste to hug Rose. They hugged each other tight, giggling as they did so.

Mowzer having finished his daily ablutions, twitched his ear at the giggles coming from the driveway, stretched his long body along the length of the bed and promptly dozed off again. Unperturbed by the noise of their new house guest and safe in the knowledge that in the very near future his belly would be rubbed by Lisa, whom he adored.

Chapter Three

Mowzer was not wrong as the first place Lisa looked for her favourite cat after greeting her friend, Rose, was in the master bedroom. She left Rose busy in the kitchen sorting out the lunch she had prepared earlier and pouring cold glasses of Kentish apple juice for the pair of them. This would morph into wine as the afternoon went by, but they always started with just a juice on a hot day. The years of togetherness and girly routines were firmly embedded in the time they spent together. They didn't huddle over teenage magazines in the afternoons anymore, they gossiped over a social media feed on their mobiles, sharing the good stuff, or if they were feeling nostalgic, they flicked through actual paper magazines, buying a selection of expensive, glossy ones just for the sheer fun of it. Lisa had lugged her holdall and suitcase up the stairs with her, intending to stake claim in the master bedroom, but as she turned at the top of the stairs, she could have sworn she saw the figurehead's hair ruffle in the cool breeze coming in from the open window in the back bedroom.

She was torn; she really wanted to dump her suitcase on the duvet in the front bedroom as it was slightly bigger and looked out over the garden to the lane. She had always wanted to sleep in this room, so she could pretend that she was the mistress of the house. However, the ship's figurehead seemed to pull her into that room. The carved figurehead was the most peculiar find that Rose had discovered in the house since she inherited the place. It was found hidden underneath the eaves when the renovations were taking place, wrapped up in an old sailcloth and seemingly squirrelled away in the loft space to keep her safe. The figurehead bore a remarkable resemblance to Rose and coincidentally carried a bouquet of roses in her hands. Too many coincidences for Rose's mum, Joan, who had refused to stay in the bedroom when she stayed last, preferring to kip on the couch downstairs away from the figurehead's steely glare. Joan was convinced that the wooden eyes of the figurehead followed her around. She swore that it was not just her eyes and sometimes she caught the wooden face moving in the same direction. Always ever so slightly, Joan was certain that the figurehead had a life of her own and moved in almost imperceptible ways that not everyone noticed. She noticed and kept away, not drawn to the quirkiness as her daughter was.

Some of Rose's friends in the village often said that they had seen Rose in the window watching them if they followed that path along the river instead of up to the folly. It was Rose's habit to watch out of the lower ground-floor window and not the top as the downstairs window seat was so comfy. So she wondered why folk thought she would stand at the upstairs window and not curl up hugging her knees, like she did when she was downstairs.

However, most people were totally unaware that Rose had spent a long time messing about with a telescope she had found in the upstairs back bedroom. The telescope was temperamental, sometimes it would focus and other times it was thoroughly broken. In the rare minutes she could get clarity in the focus she was gripped; it was always a tad blurry but familiar even if a little odd. It had been propped up so she could use it and had remained there ever since with the bed still pushed against the wall to keep it in its original position. So, she was never just standing in the window peering out, but she was at the window peering through the telescope, getting quite a distorted view of things too.

With a sigh, Lisa placed her holdall on the back bedroom bed and couldn't resist giving the figurehead lady a cheeky wink as she did so. She put her suitcase on the floor next to the bed and then crossed the landing into the master bedroom to make a fuss of her favourite boy, Mowzer. He was pretending to be in a deep sleep curled up on the bottom of the bed but cheekily opened one eye as she came into the room. An instinctive purr resonated in his throat before she had even touched him, but when she gently stroked his head, his eyes rolled in ecstasy, and he rolled onto his back. His white paws waving from side to side, his rounded white tummy displayed to his favourite friend to tickle and stroke.

Lisa was only too pleased to make a big fuss of him. She leant over him and kissed him on the top of his furry head between his ears. Mowzer enjoyed every second of the fuss and leapt up in alarm when Rose shouted up the stairs for Lisa to come down for lunch. He was very familiar with any 'food' words so made off down the stairs before Lisa, hoping to find a sprinkling of cheese on the floor from the lunch sandwiches. Cheese was a favourite snack for Rose and Mowzer, her erstwhile lunch companion, so he was first to investigate the kitchen just in case. As Lisa followed Mowzer down the stairs, the back bedroom door slammed shut. Then the master bedroom door slammed shut too. The bathroom door followed suit with an almighty slam. Then the downstairs doors banged shut one after the other. Till it was just Lisa all alone on the stairs, looking up at the darkness above and into the gloom below, the only light coming from the stained-glass windows at the side of the house. The colours of the ocean, greens and blues glinting in the sunlight as they came through the glass. The light dancing on the banisters and the wall. The same light dancing in and out of the waves in the stained glass from the windows, as the figurehead was wont to do when she was part of the ship. The Captain's ship, 'The Fortune'. Lisa clung to the banisters with one hand as she felt the swaying motion of the sea until she could take it no more and sunk down to sit on the stairs to wait the motion out. She felt exhilarated, free and so, so happy. She wiped her face dry with her sleeve as it was now dripping wet with sea water and shielded her eyes as she did so, when she moved her arm away. The colours were still on her face but there was a concerned Rose at the bottom of the stairs looking up at her, with Mowzer at her feet, face held aloft with crumbs of cheese balanced on a few whiskers.

Chapter Four

Completely unperturbed by the noise, sensations and her wet face, Lisa giggled, "I always love staying here. Did you hear? The house was saying 'Hi' to me too."

Dust motes spiralled past her hair, glistening in the sunlight and settled at her feet. She slowly made her way down the stairs holding on the banister to steady herself, until she was a couple of stairs from the bottom. There in front of her was a tiny key. The tiniest of keys.

Lisa bent down to have a closer look and lost her balance, tumbling into Rose and knocking her off her feet. Mowzer was nowhere to be seen as he was clever enough not be caught under the pair of them and had scarpered when Lisa started to lean forward towards them.

"Really, Lisa. What are you like?" said Rose, dusting herself off and pushing her friend away. "Even you can't look at your feet on the stairs. What were you looking at that was so urgent, that you couldn't wait till you were a few steps down and on the floor of the hallway?"

Lisa, after untangling herself from Rose, was now sat on the floor beside her, running her fingers through her messed up and damp hair. She stared blankly at Rose and replied vaguely, "I was looking at something, it was important to look before it disappeared, and I wanted to make sure it was real."

"What was real? What were you looking at?"

They both stared at Lisa's feet and her toes peeking out from her summer sandals, each toenail painted in a colour of the rainbow. Lisa wiggled her toes and broke into song, gleefully singing the first line of 'Somewhere over the Rainbow'. Rose grinned broadly at her friend's antics and chuckled at the array of colour that Lisa had managed to add to her toenails.

"Why, Lisa? Why all the colours?"

"It's so my toes match every outfit in my luggage. If it rains, I'll be cross as I will have to cover my beautiful handiwork up or get wet feet, won't I? I have stuffed my wheely case to the brim so I can be ready for whatever the British weather has in store for me while I stay here."

Mowzer cautiously approached Rose and Lisa in a wide circle and sniffed at Lisa's feet. He cocked his head on one side when his inquisitive nose made contact with her little toe. His little pink tongue came out and licked her toes, making Lisa giggle again. Mowzer then crept off to her side, his body crouched low to the ground, tail slowly wagging from side to side. It looked for all intents and purposes as if he was stalking a mouse.

He moved so slowly and carefully and then pounced triumphantly when he got to the wall. With one paw tense, he stretched out his claws and batted a tiny object back towards Lisa and Rose. The item glinted in the sunlight as it slid across the floor. Lisa stretched out and picked it up with a dramatic sigh.

"That's what I was looking at. What have we here? I think your Captain has given me a gift. Any idea what this key will fit, Rose?"

Rose sat beside her friend and grabbed the newel post to get up off the floor and onto her feet, and to regain her sanity as well. With a shake of her head, she stood still and silent. Then gazed in awe at her best friend, who had only been in the house for less than ten minutes and had the key Rose had been searching for in her hands. A tiny, tiny key that looked the perfect fit for the little box that had caused so much upset between her and Tom. Could it be the very same key?

Lisa stood up beside her and handed her the key. Rose held the key with her thumb and forefinger and peered closely at it, trying to ascertain if it was the right size. As she held it aloft just in front of her eyes, she looked back up the stairs. There was a distinct pile of dust on the stairs underneath the window. The pair of them traipsed back up for a closer look and then examined the wall and the window frame. This part of the house was yet to be plastered. The hallway, stairs and landing were on the list to be finished last, so all Steve's handiwork would not be wasted as there was still work to be done upstairs. If it was plastered at all; Rose liked the look of the old stone and original brickwork. The jury was still out on this decision, and she was still tuned in to any television series or articles about house makeovers for inspiration. She listened hard to all the advice that her favourite dishy celebrity architect spouted and drove Steve mad with it, quoting from him whenever there was a decision to be made, regardless of the cost.

There was a small hole in the corner of the frame where the key had been slotted in. The doors had slammed with such a velocity and with such force that the windows had actually rattled in their frames, dislodging the key and causing it to plop out. Just as her mum had foretold when she used to slam doors as a kid when she was cross. Her mum reckoned that many a time the glass had rattled so hard when she had slammed doors, she was lucky it had not cracked. Rose had a fiery temper, which took a very long time to surface as she was not quick tempered at all. It bubbled away over time, until it erupted like a fiery volcano and woe betide anyone or anything that got in her way. Thankfully the recent slamming doors had not caused much damage to her house this time, just knocking mortar loose and the concealed key out of its hiding place.

The day was warm and sunny with a very slight breeze, so Rose was sure it was the antics of her ghostly Captain, as there was nothing else that would have caused all the doors in the house to slam shut in such a way.

It took a look at the banisters before she realised that she was in direct alignment with the weird carving she had found at Christmas. Had she misread the sign from her Captain back then, thinking that the arrow was pointing at the outbuildings outside and the folly some distance away?

Chapter Five

Rose and Lisa spent the day in the garden, surrounded by the plants and flowers that Tom lovingly tended, as had generations of inhabitants of the house before him. But they didn't notice their surroundings and all Tom's hard work. They spent the time chattering incessantly and putting the world to rights between them. Their friendship had endured the distance that was between them, as they now lived too far apart for their regular evenings out. They both concluded after their second glass of wine that they should and would make more of an effort in the future. So, they made plans that Lisa should stay once a month for a long weekend or if life was busy, just overnight. Maybe just coming down on the train so they could spend the afternoon together. A long lunch, turned into a snacky dinner of comfort food, both of them plumping for 'fish finger' sandwiches, chunky chips and mushy peas after scouring the pantry and freezer for meal options. All quick to cook, very convenient and perfect after a couple of bottles of wine. They cobbled together a salad for some colour. Lisa insisted that food needed to look good on the plate, it was not meant in any way to add any healthy elements to the meal.

As the evening grew cold, they retreated back into the house, sitting in the lounge at the rear, side by side on the sofa, with a tub of chocolate ice cream between them and a spoon each. Mowzer was nowhere to be seen. When he had eaten his share of the fish from the breaded fish fingers from his favourite visitor, Lisa, he was off, leaving the women to their conversation, seeking peace and quiet away from their constant chatter.

The house was situated in a very quiet location and every time the conversation paused, Lisa looked around her in awe. All that could be heard was the river babbling noisily outside the window as it tumbled over the rocks in the middle, interrupting the smooth flow of the water.

Most of Rose's white kitchen appliances were in her utility room in the outhouse so she only had the barely perceptible low, whiny hum of her little countertop fridge, bought reluctantly when she got fed up having to cross the driveway to the utility room's fridge for milk in the winter months, just to make a cup of tea. Due to the fridge's small size, it did not break the quiet, as would a full-sized fridge-freezer in any other house. The house was static, it was as if time was paused, the house remaining still and quiet. As if the house was gearing itself up for something, waiting for a moment to pass or to play out again.

The house, as it always did, drew Lisa in, enveloping her in its gentle embrace and soothing her busy, feisty spirit. When Rose scuttled into the kitchen to clear up, wash up and make some hot chocolate for bedtime, she glanced back at her friend, ensconced in the sofa, gazing out into the encroaching darkness of the night with a smile dancing around her face. Her eyes were tired but happy.

After the excitement of the morning when they had found the tiny key, and shared their news and stories with some urgency, all was peaceful. Rose played with the little key in the pocket of her jeans. After coaxing Lisa back down the stairs and away from the house into the garden she had popped the key in her pocket. She wanted Lisa to forget it for a while. Although Rose had been keen to look in the box and she had been searching for the key for so long, it was proving to be an anti-climax for her. The fast-paced career girl that she had been, had slowed down, her pace of life had changed. She didn't rush things when she didn't need to anymore, as most of the time she didn't have to. Rose was the 'procrastination queen' these days. She hadn't told Lisa about the box and the fact that it was locked and had been since she found it, as she didn't want to force the lock, she had been only too happy to look for the key. After living in the house for some time, she knew that she needed to wait for the right time. Opening the box in a tizzy when Lisa had just arrived was not the right moment.

She wanted to savour the moment and give time for the house to respond. It would be crazy to anyone else and had seemed preposterous to Tom, who wanted to force the lock straight away to see what was inside. The glimpses of the ghosts of the past and the whispers that surrounded her seemed to appear when she needed them or as she supposed at the right time.

As she stood and deliberated these facts, she stared out into the darkness too. All the women in the house lost in their thoughts and mirroring each other. For joining them upstairs the figurehead gazed out with sightless eyes into the darkness, until a light in the far distance reflected off the carved pupils of her eyes. Her eyelids shut and then suddenly fluttered open; eyes of intense blue stared out. The outline of her body shimmered and within the shimmer right there in the blur, her body shook and bent over the sill of the window. No longer wood but to all intents and purposes real.

All the women in the house watched and waited. What were they waiting for?

Chapter Six

Rose had thrown her jeans across the armchair in the corner of her bedroom as she had been too tired to fold or put them away, when they finally got to bed in the early hours of the following morning. As she had done so the tiny key she had secreted in her pocket the previous day, flew across the bedroom floor unnoticed, before landing alongside the front window. Luckily, she really didn't have the energy to close the curtains or the old shutters either or the key would have been swept even further away into the far corner of the bedroom. The key lay there hidden once more, until Mowzer nudged it with his nose the next morning and sent it spinning across the floorboards with his paw. So, it ended up in the far corner after all, totally invisible in a pile of dust.

Lisa bounced into the room at first light, which was only a few hours since they had gone to bed, giggling with a sleepy grin resplendent on her face. She gave Rose a hefty shove to her shoulder and announced, "Yay! The first day of my holiday. Wake up, you sleepyhead. We have treasure to unlock with that key we found. Did you think I would have forgotten it for a moment and let you do it all by yourself? I found the key, does that mean the treasure is mine? All mine."

Her words trailed away, as Rose continued to sleep, before she murmured an unintelligible reply and turned over, reaching out to Mowzer as she did so. He was right there all right, presenting a joint front with Lisa, as he wanted his breakfast. When she sleepily opened one eye, Mowzer was there, in front of her, filling her vision. In her face, his eye next to hers. His nose nudged hers repeatedly. A little wet nose. To get some peace she flopped back over to her other side and there was Lisa. Then she was nose to nose with Lisa, admiring her hair all messed up. Sticking up on end, resembling a frightened cartoon character.

"Rose, get up," said Lisa impatiently. "You are so cheeky, you let me forget the key, kept me chatting about other stuff."

Satisfied that Rose was awake and would not succumb to snoozing, she paced across the room and grabbed the jeans that Rose had discarded just a few short hours before.

"Really, Rose, you are so messy. I am sure I saw you sneak it into your pocket yesterday. You thought I didn't see, didn't you? Tempting me with cake, wine and my favourite fish finger sandwiches to distract me! What are you like?"

After rummaging around in the pockets of Rose's jeans and finding nothing, she stared at her indignantly. "OK, Rose, what the bloody hell have you done with it? You haven't sneaked it away hoping I would forget, have you? Nice try, kiddo. Not me. Where is it?"

Rose sat up and then crawled to the bottom of the bed on her knees. "What do you mean? Where is the key? It's in the pocket on this side," waving her left hand in the air as she did when working out her left from her right. "You know, that left-hand side, this side," continuing to waggle her arm and hand at Lisa, pointing to the pocket.

"Stop waving at me, Rose, sit still. Here, have the jeans. Check the pockets, there is nothing there."

Rose took her jeans from Lisa and searched the pockets. All of them. She then proceeded to shake the jeans, holding the hem at the bottom of each leg. When nothing fell out, she shook them harder.

Then she slung them at Lisa and groaned.

Lisa cast her eyes heavenward at the turn of events and wailed, "Oh, Rose, we haven't lost the bloody key before we found out what it belongs to, have we? No, no, no, this is not happening."

Without saying another word to Rose, Lisa stomped out of the room and into the back bedroom. She lay down on the bed and pulled the covers over her head, suddenly feeling tired and miserable.

Rose, used to her friend's antics and sudden mood swings, took a more pragmatic approach, even though she desperately wanted to go back to sleep too. She would feed Mowzer and retrace her steps from yesterday. There was no way that Mowzer would let her sleep in.

Once Mowzer had scoffed his breakfast in no time at all, as he was not a dainty, fussy or slow eater, she opened the door, walked around the house into the garden and looked across at the table where they had spent most of the previous day. The table was empty as they had tidied, washed the crockery and wiped it down.

She could see two magpies each perched atop a chair. The chairs that were across the table from where the women had sat yesterday. Both birds were bobbing their heads up and down as if they were deep in conversation with the occupants of the empty chairs across the table.

Rose dutifully wished the birds, "Good morning, Maggie," as she was taught to do so by her mum from a child, for you must always acknowledge the presence of a magpie or bad luck would befall you. She would usually ask, 'How is your lady wife today?' but she didn't add this as she was addressing a pair of magpies. The birds then hopped across to just the one chair and both regarded her with a stare.

Feeling very silly but very sure of her actions, she started up a conversation. "Magpies are said to like shiny things? Have you taken my key by any chance? It's very shiny, you would like it."

The larger of the birds looked up at her open window and back across at her, and answered her with a guttural bark. He then took off, flying low over her head, closely followed by his companion or 'lady wife'. She watched as they circled the house and came to rest on the tiles above her bedroom window. The larger bolder bird perched atop her open window, which was ajar. The gap was not very big, so with a much louder cry and a sharp tap on the window with its beak, the bird flew off. The magpies took another low-flying loop over the rooftop of the house.

With an incredulous smile, Rose watched as they finally flew away in the direction of the folly. Surely the birds had not understood every word? With the smile on her face, she turned away from the garden and made her way back to the bedroom to search for the key once more. As she turned, she heard a familiar girlish giggle in her ear and the swish of a long skirt. The length of her companion's heavy skirt brushed the dew from the lawn at her side and her footprints were indented into the dry, dewless grass beside her as her ghostly friend walked unnoticed at her side.

Chapter Seven

Rose marched into the house. Her feet, wet from the morning dew left footprints behind her as she walked. She traipsed up the stairs once again and stuck her finger into the gap in the mortar that the key had left when it fell out the previous day. She wiggled her finger around in the hole and as she did so, she looked out across the driveway to the outbuildings. There perched on the roof tiles was the larger of the two magpies she had seen earlier, who stared right back at her. His piercing black eyes penetrated her own, until the low hum of a car approaching broke the connection and with a bob of his head he took off in the direction of the folly. The smaller bird flew around the side of the building, looking for its mate, then followed the other magpie into the distance.

Tilly had pulled up outside the outbuildings ready to start work on her most recent order. She looked up at the house, saw Rose in the window and waved, before unlocking the building and going inside. Tilly was a florist and the first to start working regularly in Rose's new rented workspace. She kept regular days and hours, but this was early for her. Instead of going back to bed, Rose got washed and dressed. She wanted a sensible chat with Tilly, she craved some normality and needed to get away from Lisa and the conundrum of the key for a while. She didn't want to do that in her PJs and dressing gown, but she was sure that Tilly wouldn't mind.

Lisa was snoring in the back bedroom, sprawled untidily across the bed, with just her bra and pants on. For she was just getting dressed when she remembered the key they had found but not done anything with, in her somewhat hungover state. The abandonment of the challenge without finding the all-important key, led to her return to bed still in an unkempt state having forgotten to get dressed or have breakfast.

Within the half-hour Rose was perched on the workbench alongside Tilly, watching her as she tackled her paperwork and ordered her stock for the new week, she was surrounded by flowers, left over from a previous order. Rose had never seen her flustered, but Tilly had overstocked for her last order and was in total disarray. Picking up a stray carnation that was on the bench alongside her, Rose trailed it between her fingers as she attempted to placate her friend.

"Tilly, this is just teething problems. Stop getting caught in the details. Were your customers happy with the wedding flowers, the bouquet, the buttonholes, the table decorations?" Without waiting for an answer, she went on, "Of course they were! All that you have to get organised and sorted is your ordering and stock system, that's it. You have just over ordered as the process is new to you, and you have flowers left over. They are fresh in here as it is cool, and you thought to put them in water. All you need to do is sell them. Or you could use them to advertise. Hey, what about advertising? You have some business cards here, some ribbon, pass them to me."

Tilly was incredulous as Rose proceeded to make mini sprays of carnations, tied them with matching ribbon and stuck a business card artfully in the middle. When she brandished the flowers up in the air triumphantly, the card fell out, so she made a small hole in the corner of the business card and threaded the ribbon through to keep it secure. While holding the second attempt very still in the air, in case something else should fall out, she chuckled.

Tilly puckered her lips together, pouted and wrinkled her nose at Rose. Her attempts were passable at best but not professional in the slightest, but the idea was sound. She snatched the flowers from Rose untied them and with careful trimming, artful cutting, adding some extra flowers and colours into the mix and fancy ribbon tie in the shape of a demure bow, she held her creation up to Rose.

"That's what I am talking about. Fantastic," said Rose. "I liked my version best, but yours look more professional, like mini bouquets. So, what are you going to do with them now?"

Tilly groaned and lay the flowers back down on the table. "What am I going to do with them now?" she echoed back at Rose.

"I reckon you should make some more with all the leftover flowers then hand them out somewhere, but where? Take a drive and see where the mood takes you. Go on, off you go, the paperwork can wait, as can your next job which isn't for a couple of days, the flowers haven't arrived yet and aren't even in your little cold room. Go on, drive out somewhere. Catch your mood, bin it and come back in a better frame of mind or not at all. Make up the rest of the flowers and be off with you."

Tilly leapt up and embraced Rose in a big hug and then turned back to her workspace with a smile.

"Thank you for being there, you. Now, be off with you, haven't you got Lisa staying here?"

With a groan, Rose spun on the spot to return to the house, as her friend had been forgotten in the moment. She was too impulsive for her own good, which was why she never got anything done. She was always flitting from one thing to another, like a moth to a light, flying fast and close but never really getting anywhere. She was completely unaware of the fact that this was her most endearing quality, her need to make sure that everyone around her was OK first. She found managing and dealing with the little details of her own activities much harder when she was not working. Without a job description and definite weekends as free time, she was adrift.

As she crossed the yard purposefully, the magpie from earlier hopped in front of her on the drive. Looking up at her, with its head on one side, the bird regarded her with intent, when she paused mid-stride, transfixed at his boldness.

The bird looked at her and then back up at the window where the key was found, making sure she followed his sight line. When he was sure that she grasped his meaning the bird took flight in a flash of black and white, up onto the roof and watched her enter the house once more.

Chapter Eight

Rose felt she had magpies on the brain, for everywhere she looked there was a magpie that morning. They were supposed to bring good luck. It was as if the magpie was trying to tell her something or telling her not to forget to find the key. Totally illogical, but why was she feeling that it was the right thing to do, trust a magpie! Laughing at herself, she entered the front bedroom and almost ran headlong into Lisa. She was on her hands and knees looking under the armchair using an old magazine to brush the wooden floorboards in front of her, to sweep up anything that was on the floor. Rose could see that it was one of Tom's expensive trade journals, but she didn't say anything, just laughed harder. She couldn't contain her mirth when she realised that Lisa was wearing a very small floral pair of knickers, with lots of lace edging, and the dainty flowers were identical to the design of the front cover of the magazine she was sweeping the floor with.

Lisa was oblivious to the cause of Rose's mirth, with her bottom bobbing up and down in the air. She was intent on her mission. She wanted to find the key, even if she had no clue what it was even for. Lisa hated to miss out on anything. Rose took a step back and waggled one of Lisa's toes lightly with her foot. This action proved to be disastrous as Lisa shrieked, leapt into the air, knocking the armchair on its side. She then hit Rose firmly on the head with the rolled magazine, until they were both face to face. Lisa red in the face with exertion and Rose a similar colour from laughing.

"I thought you were a giant mouse, you know, you big fat lout!" Lisa cried at Rose.

"You shouldn't speak like that to your host and your best friend. I really don't care though," she replied, wiping the tears of laughter from her face. "I can't take you seriously, in your bra and pants that match Tom's gardening magazine! Really, what are you like?"

"You shouldn't be laughing at me, Rose. I am being serious. I will find that key if it kills me and you nearly did, frightening me like that, pretending to be a giant mouse!"

"Let's look together, shall we? You follow the window line, and I will look over here in the corner, that way we can cover more ground."

With both of them now in opposite corners of the bedroom, Rose was spared another close encounter with Lisa's underwear. She knew there was no point asking Lisa to get dressed first, when she got an idea in her head it was better to go with it. Rose felt along the edge of the wall and almost in the corner her fingers found the key hidden in the dust. Raising it aloft like a winner's trophy she whooped with joy over the key. When she had it firmly in her hands, she couldn't resist a peek out of the window. There perched on the windowsill was her new magpie friend looking in, his head cocked to one side returning her stare before taking flight.

Lisa stood and stared as Rose mirrored the magpie's actions, dropping her head to one side before turning to face her friend.

"I would pass the key to you to keep safe, but you're not dressed yet, are you? How about you get washed and dressed? Come find me downstairs and I will show you what I think this key will fit. I have waited long enough to find the key, so another half an hour won't matter. I promise not to lose it again. Hurry up, though. It has caused no end of grief between me and Tom as he wanted to force the lock of the box. Just hurry up and I will tell you all about it."

Lisa grumbled and grabbed the tumbler of water that was by the side of Rose's bed. "I hope you have some painkillers in the bathroom as my head is pounding, not sure if it's the excitement, the fright or the wine we drank last night. Might have a soak in the bath. Do me a coffee won't you, Rose!"

She slipped into the bathroom with a wry grin and closed the door very gently. Holding the key very tight, Rose went downstairs to retrieve the tin box from where she had hidden it from Tom, at the very back of the pantry, behind the old crockery. The last place a man would look, she thought, and she was right. Tom had been quietly searching for the box ever since she found it and had refused to open it.

She hoped that whatever it was, it was connected to the house, the Captains and the mysterious ladies of the house. It could be stuffed full of cash, and if it was, she would be disappointed. Although the money would come in handy, she was looking for something more personal. Something in keeping with the house. It seemed like a lady's possession which was why she didn't want Tom to open it.

When she opened the pantry door, reaching in to move the old crockery, she felt a presence behind her. She knew it wasn't Lisa as she could hear her moving about in the bathroom upstairs. The water sloshing about in the bathtub. She pushed the breakfast bowls to one side and pulled the box towards her. When the box was clutched close to her chest, she heard a small sigh.

She laid the tin box carefully on the work surface of the kitchen and tried the key in the tiny lock. It fitted perfectly. She turned the key in the lock and lifted the lid to look inside.

Then she felt a warm breath on her neck as if someone was holding her gently, looking over her shoulder, checking that the contents were just as they should be.

Chapter Nine

Typically, everything in the house that had previously been hidden away was always found wrapped in sail cloth to keep the contents safe and weathertight. The old wooden figurehead was found wrapped up tight in an old sailcloth in the eaves and gave them all such a fright when they found it, as they thought it was a dead body until it was unwrapped. This box was not an exception to the rule, although the tin had been exposed to the elements while buried in the roots of the old beech tree. The contents were indeed wrapped in an old sail cloth.

Rose teased open the wrappings with her fingers, all the while feeling the breath of her ghostly companion on her neck. She could smell the essence of her, a warm heady fragrance of roses mixed in with the fresh summery scent of a garden. She breathed in, instinctively, but held her breath too long, making her head swim and her vision blurry.

The scent was cloying now, very overpowering and she had to force herself to breathe naturally. *In and out, in and out,* she told herself and looked down at her hands now hidden in the folds of the sailcloth. Rose had dressed that morning in a short-sleeved summer blouse with very short puff-type sleeves that covered her shoulders. Her arms were bare, as were her fingers. She had not yet put her treasured gold band on her finger, taking it off as she always did when she washed, balancing it on a little saucer on the windowsill of the bathroom.

But the hands she was looking at deep in the folds of the cloth, had rings on most fingers. Dainty rings with very small stones embedded in the shiny gold and silver bands. The hands were small and delicate. The arms were encased in white, pure white with a little frill at the ends, covering the wrist in a puff of lace. The sleeves tied at the wrist with a tiny pink ribbon. Her nails were neatly manicured. Rose continued to breathe deeply and looked hard at the hands in front of her. She could no longer feel the breath on her neck, she was enveloped in the presence of the lady instead. Her breath was shallow, and the sighs and murmurs coming from her were not her own.

These hands gently uncovered what lay within, reverently with great care. Individually wrapped but on the very top was a brooch, silver in the shape of a boxed bow with a rose engraved in the front. A faint hue of pink was all that was left on the rose itself, as she turned it over and her fingers lightly tapped the back. Alongside the brooch was another package; she drew this close to her and clenched it tight. Rose felt the tears begin to fall and she was overcome by a profound sense of sadness. The package was returned to the box and uncovered in the same way. Within the folds was a silver pocket watch, very well worn and loved. She picked it up, the weight of it familiar in her hands. It was tactile to touch. Searching in the folds for more objects, she came across a bundle of old photographs and drawings tied together with a length of pink ribbon.

The same pink ribbon that was at her wrists. Her head spun as her brain processed the information. The fact of the matter. The same ribbon. *The same ribbon.* The words rang in her head, over and over again.

Her vision blurred as she stared at the grainy faded photograph at the top of the pile. It was a house. The ribbon dissected the photograph into two halves One side was familiar to her and the other side was odd. Very strange. She brought the photo to her eyes to get a closer look, catching another glimpse of pink. The pink ribbon and lace blurred into one, as if someone was stirring a pot of paint. The colours swirled together in a never-ending circle, never completely merging, the shade of pink staying constant.

Her tears were drying now and as her head continued to pound, she dropped the photos and they fell to the floor.

"Oh, oh, my!" The cry reverberated around the kitchen and echoed along the passage. It was loud. It was shrill.

Through the pink haze she stared at the floor, tried to focus on the flagstones of the kitchen and then sunk to her knees making her dress rustle against her.

A dress, a dress, her head told her, contradicting that very same fact for she had dressed in jeans that morning. Blue denim jeans, with the obligatory split in the knee that drove her mum mad.

She was wearing a dress…

"Oh, oh, oh…what am I to do!" she cried in a shrill voice that was not her own, laced with tears and emotion. The cry got louder until she picked up the bundle of photographs once more and held them tight.

It was there, that Lisa found her friend, on her knees in the kitchen, in tears, holding the package close to her chest. She could see the tin box was open on the countertop behind Rose. She wanted to be angry that Rose had opened the box without her, but the cries and wails that she heard so clearly from upstairs stopped her. There was plenty of time to be cross later, she told herself under her breath. Lisa crouched down beside her and holding Rose tight, gently lifted her to her feet, slowly propelled her into the back room and sat her upright in the armchair. Taking the bundle from her hands she placed them on the mantelpiece. Safe, but out the way and then started to massage Rose's hands. They were white and freezing cold. Her eyes were glazed over but she hadn't said a word, not a word since her cries had stopped. It was so unlike Rose that Lisa started to get worried.

With the brisk massage to her hands, the colour was starting to come back, and the light was returning to her eyes once more.

Then Rose blinked hard a couple of times, which was all it took. She was right there again, holding Lisa's hands in her own before wiping what remained of the tears from her eyes.

Chapter Ten

It took a while before Rose felt herself again. Lisa hovered in the background and gave her the space that she needed. She didn't ask any questions, just brought the box into the back room and sat it on the mantlepiece for Rose to re-examine when she felt better.

Rose was expecting her friend to be cross with her for trying the key in the lock and opening the box without her, but she wasn't at all. This was why they had remained best friends for ages. They understood and accepted each other without question. Always a lot of humour, fun and laughter when they were together, but the serious issues were never sidestepped and discussed in every minute detail but only when the time was right for the both of them.

Lisa escaped to the garden away from the drama and wandered around the flower beds, resplendent with big showy roses. The roses were the main focus of the garden and Tom's pride and joy. Tom was slowly restoring the garden to its former glory and was uncovering hidden paths and some stone features. The weekend before he left, he uncovered a pond that had been filled in and allowed to silt up over the years. The pond was in an odd place in the garden, tucked away at the side. Tom was excited to have found it, but never liked messing about with water and the pond looked like it was going to be huge. Too big for him to be comfortable with. One of his old school friends was mad about water sports and spent his working life as a landscape gardener like Tom. His speciality was water features, ponds, pools and natural pools for swimming that were becoming all the rage and very trendy. Duncan was very busy, but Tom was going to seek him out to ask him to restore the pond with him. Or if he asked him right, do the whole job for him, so he could concentrate on his roses.

Tom spent a while researching the likely size of the pond he had uncovered and trudged around for ages looking for clues. For once, Rose had not joined him. She did not have his passion for the garden but enjoyed it looking its best and loved spending time out there. An easy to maintain garden suited her. So, she thought a gardener was her ideal partner. Tom was forever, pruning, snipping and spraying natural insecticide at the roses to keep them at their best and disease at bay. Rose liked the roses when they were in a vase and loved arranging them to show them off at their best, without having to do any work. She had surprised Tilly and herself with her rudiment floristry skills and she knew she could do better with the right training and dedication, if she wished.

While wandering aimlessly, Lisa found herself at the edge of the pond. The corner of the pond that Tom had uncovered days earlier. It was in a rather shady spot, an odd place for a pond but looking up, she could see that the trees had grown over it and just needed to be trimmed back into place. A large pile of bricks stood in the far corner of the garden, partially obscured by overgrowth, so at first sight it was just a grassy mound. It caught her eye, so she walked over to the mound and saw that there was not just one mound but several… The bricks open to the elements were weathered. Traces of mortar remained, with a residue of blackness on some. Lisa pulled back some of the waist-height overgrown weeds and then some more when she saw she was making progress. As she tore at the weeds with her bare hands, she wrinkled her nose in distaste. Surely someone was not having a bonfire on such a lovely day. Looking around for the source of the smell and the offending bonfire, she concluded that there wasn't any smoke. The smell was coming from the bricks themselves. As she uncovered the lower half of the mound, she could see blackened bricks with a thick layer of soot on them.

Moving across to the other mounds she made small indentations, stripping away the ragged, matted undergrowth to see if the mounds were identical. They were. Then there were more as she ventured further, underneath and behind the trees bordering the property. On the neighbouring marshland where Rose's neighbour grazed his sheep, Lisa found more builder's rubble. It was not recent though, there were large lumps of stone masonry from numerous window and door frames. Under the hedge itself were large lengths of wood, which could have been heavy beams at one time before the weather had taken its toll.

Lisa was really having fun now, getting messy, dirty and losing track of time. She wiggled into the undergrowth and into a tightly knitted copse of trees. Hawthorn, she guessed as the prickles dug into her skin. She reached for a darker lump of wood that was entirely hidden and obscured by the trees. Something cold and wet jumped up and into her legs. She immediately screamed and ran out from under the trees. Catching her breath and telling herself not to be so silly, she peered into the gloom, to be met by a pair of eyes blinking back at her from inside the head of a very large toad.

Clutching her throat and raising her eyes to the heavens, she grinned back at the toad.

"Judging by the size of you, this area hasn't been touched or disturbed for years. What can all this be? Why is it here? Does it belong to the Captain's House, or has it been dumped here years or centuries ago? The bricks look familiar. I must ask Rose."

She looked down at her watch and gasped at the time she found displayed. She extracted herself further from the brambles that had somehow attached themselves to her cotton summer trousers and brushed herself down. "I must check on Rose, I hope she is all right!"

When she got back to the house, she raced into the back room to check on Rose, but she wasn't there. Mentally chiding herself for thinking Rose should have been where she left her, for she was not an inanimate object, she called out.

"Rose, where are you? Is everything all right? Are you OK?"

There was no answer. She looked across at the mantelpiece where she had left the box. The tin box was sat there where she had left it but now it was all locked up with the key in the lock. The key had a strip of faded pink ribbon tied in a bow on its circular end. The bundle of photographs and pictures were missing, as was Rose.

Chapter Eleven

There was no answer from within the house. Lisa raced through every room looking for her friend. She knew that Rose had wanted to be alone after the weirdness in the kitchen, so she had acceded to her request for solitude, but she desperately wished she had insisted that she stayed with her when her search proved fruitless.

It was summertime, so she couldn't tell if Rose had gone somewhere for a wander, like she had earlier, but she hadn't seen her on her way back. There were no clues to be found, as it was very unlikely she would have grabbed a jumper or coat as the day was pleasantly warm. Nothing was visibly missing. Her car was still parked up in the driveway when she looked out into the garden and there was nothing that indicated Rose had been outside, when she came in through the garden.

On the way back down the stairs she peeked out of the side window at the outbuildings and noticed that the door to the main building looked ajar. It was hard to tell from the angle she was looking from, so she went to check. Sure enough, the door was swaying in the gentle breeze and Mowzer was sprawled outside, dozing in the sunshine. He just blinked at her and completely ignored her when she whispered, "Have you seen your mistress, you?"

Lisa couldn't help but giggle as she had talked to a toad earlier and now, she was addressing the cat. *Must be the air,* she thought as she pushed the big door open and strode purposefully inside. The air was cooler inside and smelt of the fresh flowers that Tilly and Rose had been preparing earlier in the day. The place was empty. Everyone's workspace was tidy and gleaming with the exception of Tilly's which looked as if she had left in a hurry, indeed she had. On a mission to give away her flowers, to advertise her new business on sheer impulse.

Lisa reached down and picked up a flyer for a wedding fayre that was being held locally in the nearby town. She guessed that was where Tilly was heading to, but where was Rose?

Mowzer had followed Lisa in and calmly made his way past her and up the stairs in the corner that led to the loft space in the eaves of the old building. The stairs had been casually roped off, to stop anyone going upstairs as the space was not for rent and Rose had not yet decided what to use the area for. The stairs were rickety and very dusty, but she knew that this had to be an illusion of sorts, as Steve was very thorough in his work and Rose trusted him impeccably. Nevertheless, she held onto the handrail and made her way carefully upstairs following Mowzer, who was padding along in front of her waving his black tail with its little white tip in the air as he strode.

"Woo hoo, anyone there?" she cried as she got to the top and looked around into the loft space. There was no answer, she couldn't see anyone, just a heap of old sail cloths taking up most of the space. Mowzer clambered over the cloth, picking his way around the obscure lumps and bumps and jumped down. He was greeted by a wail of alarm.

"Ah, what the hell is that?" Rose was crouched at the back of the loft space gazing out of the small round window that faced back towards the house. Standing up, she dusted herself down and picked up Mowzer with a grin.

"What you up to, little man? You shouldn't scare me like that!"

Mowzer answered with a loud purr and a contented little squeak and then wriggled to be put down. As Rose placed him carefully back on the floor, she saw Lisa on the other side of the space. Noticing her grim expression, she realised she had worried her friend and guessed that she had been looking for her. She knew she had been deep in thought and when she was thinking that hard she wouldn't have heard anyone calling her.

She held the bundle of photographs in her hand and used it to wave Lisa around the edge of the covered objects taking up most of the room.

"I don't expect you to clamber over all this, like Mowzer, but you have got to come over here and look at the view from this window and then look at this photograph. You will never guess what I have found."

Lisa joined her friend at the window and took in the view from it. She could see the side of the house. The outbuildings were set at an odd angle from the house, due in part to the path of the river that ran alongside the property, which meandered instead of flowing a straight course. They got a good view from up there of the back of the property. The garden surrounding the back of the house was unkempt at best as it ran alongside the river with its many small tributaries flowing towards the sea. The grass was cut back from time to time but there wasn't really space for any seating or anything else. The sightline from the house to the river and beyond made it one-of-a-kind and Rose hadn't walked along the side of the house for a long time. She walked the footpath on the way to the beach or to the folly but not the perimeter of the building. The last person to do so would have been Steve when he checked the brickwork after the winter weather.

The house rose above the river and looked as if it had always been there, solid and secure in the landscape that surrounded it.

They could see a definite shadow running alongside the house, which cast darkness on the water flowing below. The shadow continued beyond, running in a straight line as if the house continued and was twice its size. The Captain's House was small in comparison to the shadow that was cast across the water.

As the sun retreated behind a bank of cloud, the shadows remained long and dark across the water, showing the shadow of a larger footprint of a property that simply wasn't there.

Lisa and Rose stood transfixed at the window until the shadows cleared as the sun popped out from behind the clouds again. Without a word, Rose passed the photograph in her hands to Lisa. There was a grainy image of a house in her hands, very faint. The house looked remarkably similar to her Captain's House, but it was twice the size.

Chapter Twelve

"Is that why there is so much stuff stashed away in the outbuildings, Rose?" asked Lisa as she lifted the edge of the sailcloth to reveal an assortment of furniture, books, lamps and other random items that were part of the estate.

"I have no idea. There is a similar mountain of crockery and cutlery in the back of the big pantry cupboard in the kitchen. Not looked closely at the cutlery but it looked very tarnished. I suppose it could be silver, couldn't it? I can't reach most of it. I can't really believe that I am still discovering the secrets of the house. I suppose if I had been working, I would have been running around like a headless chicken at the weekends, looking everywhere for stuff to do, but as I am no longer working full time, I have got very 'lackadaisy' with everything and taking it all at a slower pace. Some of this stuff was downstairs and shifted up here by Steve and Tom when we got the downstairs ready for the Studio Open Day. You are not going to be bored while you are here unless you want to be, Lisa."

Lisa wasn't really listening to Rose; she was rummaging amongst the jumble of stuff. She had made a couple of piles already. A pile of very old books, brown and caked in dust. A couple of gas lamps and pretty shades.

"What have we here?" she yelled in excitement, something wrapped up in another layer so must be exciting. "Give me a hand, Rose." The item was massive, completely flat and wrapped up in waxed paper tied with brown string. It was very heavy. Together, they dragged it over to the wall and propped it up. Lisa tried to tear the paper but it wouldn't rip. So, Rose pulled at the string, which had lost its strength as it aged. With a quick frustrated tug, the string broke and Rose peeled back the paper. "I reckon it's another painting, Rose. If it is, mum and dad would be so pleased as they reckon there should be more somewhere. I did promise to ask you. There should be a portrait in the house somewhere, my mum is sure of it. Oh, do you reckon this is it?"

"It is so heavy, perhaps it is a carving or another part of the Captain's ship. Pull your side away from the front."

The brown paper fell away from the item, and they saw themselves reflected in a very old mirror. An ornate wooden frame with gold gilding, giving it an extra sparkle. The mirror looked extremely old, and their reflections were not perfect. Instead, they were very dim.

"Wow, oh wow, Rose. Look at this gorgeous thing. We have to get this back to the house. Do you think it was the over-mantel mirror? It is rather big for that, isn't it? Let's get it back to the house and have a proper look. We can't swing a cat here, can we, eh! Mowzer, where are you going?"

Mowzer trotted off down the stairs when he saw them trying to manoeuvre such a large item in such a small space. Rose was all for dragging it along on its corner, but Lisa, coming from a family of art restorers knew that this could prove disastrous and damage the mirror. Covering the mirror with the brown paper again but without the string as it was too brittle to be much use, they manhandled it out of the loft space to the top of the stairs. They were arguing about who should go down backwards when they heard scrabbling from down below.

Scrabbling and scraping noises across the flagstones. Then a plaintive loud meow and an answering woof of a reply.

Rose and Lisa grinned at each other. They knew exactly who was downstairs, Mickey and his trusty canine sidekick, Bert.

"Just in time, Mickey, come on up," invited Rose.

"Oh er missis, that sounds like my Rose, but it could be a wanton woman wanting her wicked way with me!" Mickey chuckled. "Identify yourself."

"Really, Mickey, now is not the time for you to share your sexual fantasies, you could be my father! This is heavy. Give us a hand, won't you?"

Mickey looked up and saw the girls grappling with a wrapped object at the top of the stairs. "Oh, what have you there? Give me the end, why don't you, and then you can show me."

Carefully the three of them made their way down the stairs. With a whistle to Bert, Mickey encouraged them to continue walking and take it straight over to the house before they set it down.

They crossed the yard like a six-legged crab and took the mirror into the back room and stood it up against the sofa, missing the internal walls and doorways by a whisker. Bert danced around their legs as they did so, trailing his lead alongside him, barking excitedly with every step.

Mickey unwrapped the mirror at the first opportunity he got, while Lisa and Rose looked on, sharing his excitement and hugging each other with the joy of it.

When Rose realised she had left the outbuilding unlocked and the bundle with the photographs next to the window, she rushed out to retrieve the bundle and lock up. Looking up at the window from the drive, she saw a familiar face looking down at her.

There, looking through the glass at her, lounging on the internal round brick sill, was Mowzer. His body moulded in the semi-circular arc. At the window, she fondled his ears and tickled his neck in his favourite spot and looked over the top of his body at the house once again. The shadow from the building was as it should be. The ghostly vision of the bigger house was not visible this time.

She turned away to pick up the bundle and saw a rectangle in the dust where the bundle had been, but it was no longer there. She looked underneath the sailcloth and found the precious bundle, turning it over in her hands to find the photograph that was at the top. It was very dusty. She wiped it with her hand to clear the dust. The image remained but was hardly there.

It was fading before her eyes as a soft sigh sounded behind her.

Chapter Thirteen

The soft sighs followed Rose around for several days afterwards, tangible signs that the lady with the pink ribbons remained at her side. If she sat down, she felt the slight movement and thud of someone sitting next to her on the sofa. In bed, there was a presence with her, a small indention in the mattress when she got up. It took a while for her to feel comfortable with her ghostly companion. She was very happy that Lisa was staying in the house with her, as she felt that her invisible acquaintance was watching and waiting for her to be on her own again.

The mirror had been carried into the front room, which she was using as her dining room. Rose and her family had enjoyed mealtimes at the table at Christmas time, but she was not using the table regularly, just for special occasions. It was the last room on her renovation plan, and it just didn't have the homely feel. It always felt cold and unwelcoming, as if something was missing and something was not quite right. Rose never spent much time there. If she wanted to look out of the window she went upstairs and sat in the old armchair in the corner of her bedroom near the window. She never looked out from downstairs, not even if she was expecting a guest.

As a consequence, the front room was becoming a bit of a junk room as anything she found that was remotely suitable for the room, was just dumped there. Whereas the back room felt comfortable and homely from the first time she walked in when she was looking around the house that had been left to her from her great old aunt, unsure of what to do with it. When she found anything for that room, she immediately put it in its 'rightful place'. The Captain's hat on the mantelpiece or the little sofa she found when she first went into what was now her utility building, which fitted the room perfectly, although it was a real pickle to get it back into the house again. It was here that she placed her first Christmas tree in her new home. There was not as much space in the back room as there was at the front, but she had the bay window to add into the equation in the back room. The front room was empty but for all the boxes and other stuff cluttering up the space, with just the table and chairs to serve a useful purpose. A Christmas tree would have looked stunning in the window and would have been seen from the lane and admired by her neighbours, but it didn't feel right to put it there.

However, the mirror was stood up against the wall and Rose was waiting for Steve to pop in to hang it there or over the fireplace. It was too big for the chimney, really, and would look a bit daft. She knew Steve would have the best ideas and wasn't going to do anything with her amazing find without asking him for his opinion. But Lisa was not in the same mindset. She had let herself into Steve's storeroom and office that he shared with Tom, found the right tools and wanted them to do the job themselves. 'Why wait and ask a man, when you can do it yourself?' was one of her mantras. It had taken a while, but Rose talked her out of her excitable, impulsive, harebrained ideas for the room; she didn't want to be bothered with it. She was happy not to 'dress' the room as Lisa wanted to, just have the table and chairs there for when she had guests or needed to use it and leave it at that. She even closed the door unless she was going in. The door was kept firmly shut. All the other internal doors in the house were left wide open.

Lisa had given up trying to talk her into using the room but managed to get the mirror in there and talk Rose round to putting it back either on a wall or on the chimney breast. She had sourced curtains, tiebacks, cushions, table cloths, lamps, napkin rings one afternoon on the internet, even popping them into the virtual shopping baskets onscreen. However, when she wanted to buy them, they were discarded as Rose changed the subject or was unfazed and had usually wandered off.

Unusually, Lisa would find Rose in the front dining room when she looked for her. She was quiet and appeared steady when she confronted her and asked what she was doing, but it was so out of character for her to wander in so frequently.

Steve was really bemused when he arrived to see Rose standing at the front window when he arrived, so he knocked at the front door instead of going round to the back as her friends and family did.

A laughing Lisa answered the front door, though not Rose as he expected.

"What's the reason you are rapping on the front door, Steve?" she enquired as she opened the door wide for him to enter the hallway.

"Well, I could see Rose in the front room so thought she would have flung the door open to greet me before I had chance to knock, but she hasn't. What's so funny? Have I got something between my teeth, or have you girls been gossiping about me? Why the laughter? Tell me, Lisa."

Lisa took a step back with the door still in her hands, her smile faded, and her giggles stopped abruptly mid-flow. She looked over her shoulder at Rose who had followed her friend up the passage to see who was at the door from the back room, where Lisa and Rose had been huddled over the laptop looking for curtain fabrics, when a wrong search word had brought something completely different onto the screen, making them laugh. Steve peered past Lisa at Rose.

Then the dining room door swung open suddenly and a rush of cold air spilled into the hallway. Steve shook his head, blinked a couple of times to check his vision and double checking that Rose was indeed standing behind Lisa, and giving Lisa a little shove to move her out of the way, stepped into the dining room.

The room was empty. It was so cold that there was moisture on the windowpanes. An arrow had been drawn in the wetness, to the right in the direction of the fireplace and outside wall. It looked as if it had been drawn with a finger, where Steve thought he had seen Rose.

Rose and Lisa followed him in and he turned to explain himself, taking in Rose's bright yellow T-shirt and cut-off denim shorts. At the window it looked like she was wearing a white dress with pink ribbons at the neckline and cuffs. Lisa stood by the side of him for a closer look at the arrow, which was quickly fading as the temperature was warming up significantly, until Rose entered the room and the chill descended once more.

Rose avoided Steve's questioning look and cast her gaze at the mirror sitting on the bare floorboards leaning up against the freshy plastered wall. The hem of a white dress and a pair of black buttoned-up boots weren't next to her in the mirror, they were in the very same place her bare feet should be.

There was no reflection of Rose. Just Steve, Lisa and her ghostly companion, not her. Rose clutched Steve tight. He responded by putting his arm nonchalantly around her shoulders and pulling her in close. As Steve embraced her, the black boots disappeared and the mirror showed her true reflection again, but the tiny boots and a flash of the white dress reappeared moments later standing behind her.

Lisa pointed at the fireplace and there at the bottom of the chimney in the fire grate was another Captain's hat, very battered, torn and extremely dusty.

Another Captain's hat!

Chapter Fourteen

The mirror was still sat on the floor untouched when Steve left.

He had spent the whole afternoon with Lisa and Rose talking about the dining room at the front of the house. Steve had plastered some of the brickwork earlier on in the year, leaving some parts exposed to show the fabric of the building. They had all agreed to leave the wall containing the chimney breast till last and it still bore some remnants of the previous wallpapers. Steve had peeled a number of layers off in several places and you could see different fashions reflected in the papering. Steve had stopped peeling off every layer and left this for Rose to see, when he had got to this green shade. This particular wall seemed to have had an additional layer of green wallpaper. Wallpaper of this vintage could contain arsenic which had helped to produce the stunning deep green but rendered the paper poisonous as a result. It was unfortunate as this was the wallpaper Rose and Lisa liked the best. It was vibrant and added some cheer to the unloved room. Steve had suggested that the design could be reproduced by Ashley and was waiting to hear her pricing. He was waiting for Rose's final decision.

When the beech tree had fallen earlier on in the year, the room felt different, not so dark as it was not in the semi-permanent shadow of the old tree anymore. Rose still did not venture in there much and Steve had only returned that afternoon on the insistence of Lisa, not Rose. It was a project that Lisa loved and once the constant chatter of old friends meeting again died down, she set herself up as the unofficial project manager of the unfinished, unloved room. Lisa could not believe that her friend was being so odd about this room.

Lisa retrieved her laptop from the back room and set it up on the table and proceeded to flood poor old Steve with her ideas. His head was awash with ideas when he left and the decision on what to do with the chimney breast wall was still unmade, because he was waiting to hear how much his suggestion would cost Rose. Steve was concerned that some of the recent plastering had fallen off and cracked in the corners adjoining the outer wall. The moisture that had formed more than once on the inside of the glass when they were talking around the table bothered him too. Nothing more was going to get done in that room until he, George and James had a good look at the brickwork and the window frames to assess what was going on, despite the pleading and cajoling from Lisa.

He noticed that Rose was very quiet, not joining in very much, only speaking if answering a question and she sat very still, fondling the newly discovered Captain's hat in her hands, stroking away the dust and dirt and bending the hat back into the correct shape again. When she first picked it up from the fireplace, it looked as if it needed a good soak to get all the ingrained dirt of the centuries out of the hat. It was tatty and very dishevelled. It had not left Rose's hands, not had that good soak, but it looked so much better, having regained its shape and lustre. The hat baffled Steve and after nearly seeing Rose in two places at once, he was really bothered by it.

He was not cheered by the sight of this Captain's hat as he was by the one she had found on her first visit. The new hat emitted waves of sorrow and sadness. He could see why Rose felt an indifference to this room. A definite disinterest in how it looked, which was astonishing in its contrast to the sunny optimism and natural curiosity she had for the rest of the house, outbuildings and the mysterious folly that was sat in the far reaches of her grounds.

He had tried to catch Lisa on her own to share his concerns for Rose, but everywhere Lisa went Rose followed. Soundlessly Rose followed her friend when she stood up to see Steve out. That afternoon it was as if he was surrounded by a gaggle of women all the time, but only Lisa was talking. He was sure he saw another woman or two on the periphery of his vision constantly watching, listening but taking no part in the conversation. Rose was the only visible participant of these other women, who were silent and watching.

Knowing that Tom was away and sensing that he was not going to get Lisa on her own, he changed tack and broke Rose away from Lisa. At the door he pulled Rose away on the pretence of looking at something in the garden. Lisa wandered back in to continue her internet shopping and research on the dining table, and he threw his arm around Rose's shoulders for the second time that day. He walked her out to the edges of the garden where the roots of the beech tree still lay, upended in the dirt. With the lane behind them, they both stared back at the house.

Rose leaned into Steve for comfort when her vision blurred and when it cleared, she saw a different house in front of her. She was struck mute and turning to see what Steve thought, she saw the Captain standing at her side, not Steve. Her hands were empty again as the hat was on the Captain's head once more. With a smile and a nod, the Captain looked back at his property, encouraging Rose to do so.

When she felt a slight squeeze and looked back at the Captain for reassurance, he took her in his arms and held her tight.

"You are so cold, you are. So very cold," the Captain said in a lilting, hesitant tone. "You are so cold, Rose. Look at me, Rose, please. What have you done with that hat?"

"The hat is on your head, my darling," replied Rose.

Steve repeated his earlier statement and question. "You are so cold, Rose. Look at me, Rose, please. What have you done with that hat?"

Looking away and then at her empty hands then back at Steve not the Captain, Rose felt a sob at the back of her throat but caught it just in time, by taking a deep breath.

She was silent, but the sound of crying could be heard in the summer breeze.

Chapter Fifteen

The mirror looked forlorn propped up against the wall of the front room.

It wasn't a cold night, as the weather had been warm and fair, just a tad chillier than the daytime temperature. However, there was a layer of moisture on the glass. Everything was damp, the table, chairs and the piles of stuff that had been dumped there waiting for another day.

You could not see in or out of the room as there was condensation on both sides of the glass, inside and out. The door, which Rose carefully shut on the way upstairs to bed, was wide open and pawprints could be seen on the floor. A little trail of pawprints to the fireplace where Mowzer was fast asleep curled up in the new Captain's hat.

The only light in the room was moonlight, which was reflected in the wetness. Mowzer was snug and warm but didn't quite fit inside this hat as he did in the bigger hat that he favoured for a sleeping place. He was a young cat now, not a kitten, so he was fast losing his favourite hiding and cosy sleeping nooks.

Mowzer stirred and looked up when he heard his mistress walking above him. When she continued to pace across the floor from one side of the house to the other, he sat up, disgruntled. His hackles rose and his tail grew fluffier when he realised that the footsteps were not Rose's. They were dainty but solid steps, clad in boots, not the shuffling sound that he was used to in the night from Rose's feet clad in her fluffy slippers when she padded into the bathroom to the toilet.

He crept out from the hat and looked up. He shook his head from side to side when it got wet, as the condensation started to form big drips. The drip, drip, drip was accompanied by tap, tap, TAP as the boots tapped their way downstairs.

After gazing with distaste at the ceiling, he sat with his head on one side until the footsteps came right beside him into the room. He blinked in the darkness and looked to see who had joined him. Seeing no one but sensing someone there, he tentatively stretched his head and wrinkled his nose to have a sniff. The strong smell of boot polish from the tip of the ladies' boot was all he discovered at first, but the swish of a skirt brushed the top of his head and then a faint hint of perfume, lightly scented but very fragrant. He turned his head towards the mirror, and he saw his new companion clearly through the reflection. He liked what he saw and curled around her legs, claiming her as his own.

She bent down and caressed his head, tickling him under the chin with her fingers. Then sank to the floor, sat down and pulled him in close, burying her face into his fur and holding him tight. She cried silently at first but as her pent-up emotions released, she started to sob. Mowzer crept into her lap and curled up tight, letting her tears fall onto his fur.

The house resonated with the sound of the quiet sobbing and the gentle, reassuring purring for most of the night until the dawn broke.

Chapter Sixteen

Lisa reluctantly left Rose after her short holiday without getting the opportunity to speak to Steve again and not finalising the front room of the house. She did, however, manage to get Rose to order all the items she had selected for the room on the internet. A couple of items had arrived the very next day and were stacked up in the corner of the room, after being opened by an enthusiastic Lisa and a disinterested Rose. Tufts of Mowzer's fur were stuck to the edges of the boxes where the tape had been partially peeled off, as the ever-inquisitive cat had circled the boxes, looking for a way inside and another place to sleep.

The new Captain's hat had vanished and after much searching by an increasingly flustered Rose it remained missing.

Rose was not herself; she was on the edge of tears most days and Lisa hated leaving her, but she had a busy time coming up at work and even with her zany ways could not manage to be in two places at once no matter how much she tried.

Rose and Lisa had visited Val for one of her afternoon cream teas that she was becoming famed for locally. Lisa had managed to have a quiet word in her ear about her concerns for Rose. She didn't believe for one minute that it was because she was missing Tom or because Tom had stretched his holiday for an extra couple of weeks. Val thought it very odd that Tom was staying away from his beloved roses in the garden of the Captain's house in the height of the summer. Rose did her best to follow the handwritten instructions that Tom had stuck on the front of the little fridge with a magnet, for the care of the garden. She watered the plants daily, looking out for any of the pests and diseases that roses were prone to, which he had written in capitals and underlined.

It seemed that Tom loved the garden more than Rose herself. Some evenings he called for a chat, but most of the time they just texted. The texts always seemed garden related and when confronted by Lisa's aversion to the constant topic of conversation, Rose seemed to paste a silly grin on her face and retort, "Tom, tells me that I am the most important 'Rose' in the garden." It was a real bone of contention between them when Lisa revealed that of course she was the most important Rose as she was the one that owned the bloody garden, and he wouldn't get his hands on the beloved garden if he didn't treat her with any importance, would he!

Val would always keep a motherly eye on Rose and had done since they first met in the London cake shop when Rose was still working in the office around the corner. Rose had stayed with Val while Steve and his friends made her new home habitable. Her mum, Joan and Val were now very good friends and Rose often wondered if she was a detour on the way to Val's for her mum now instead of her mum just coming to see her. Her mum and dad had made firm friends in the village too and Mickey and her dad, Pete, were as thick as thieves when they were together. She had wondered if her mum and dad were considering moving to the area, as she caught her dad looking at the properties for sale with Mickey several times. Both times, they were looking at the new apartments now up for sale in the building that used to be 'The Ship' pub.

The consortium that was Trevor and his nephew, Mike, had sold off all the property they owned, which included the old pub when they hadn't been able to dupe Rose into selling any of her land or property, especially the land that bordered theirs. The sale of the consortium's property in the area was as sneaky as was the acquisition of the property and acreage in the first place. The village were totally unaware that anything had changed, until a fleet of different livered vehicles had arrived to finish the renovation of the pub. Then the whole project slowed down and local tradesmen were called upon to help complete the work and add some local flair. The completed apartments were delightful; a little overpriced for the area, but that was only because the specification was so much higher than the previous consortium had been working to. Several of the locals had looked around the apartments and were contemplating buying them. The ground floor was set to be a coffee shop with a small lunch menu. It was ironic that the pub that had been the hub for the men of the village was set for a complete change and would be a hub for predominantly the women and children in the future. The land at the back had been fenced off into small gardens for the apartments and the car park was to be shared by the new residents and customers of the little shop. It was a pleasing finale to the debacle of the demise of the much-loved pub.

Rose was not sure if she wanted her parents to sell the family home she had grown up in. Maybe she should have converted her outbuildings into an annexe for her mum and dad, but when she raised this missed opportunity, her mum berated her and stated that she was not old enough to live in with her daughter. She would never wish to impose on her daughter's privacy like that, unless she was very elderly and infirm. Going on to say that she sincerely hoped she would be fit as a fiddle, much like the old aunt that had left the family the Captain's house in the first place, and never get frail enough to need nursing and constant care. Her mum was hoping that fitness into old age was a family trait that would be continued.

Rose wrinkled her nose at the suggestion that should she ever want to wander around the house or garden stark naked as the mood took her, she should not have to worry about her parents cramping her style. After this statement, she made a mental note not to use her key when she visited her parents again, there was something all too familiar with the way her mum flaunting the sheer delight of abandoning ones clothes and walking around naked that worried her. She didn't mind what they got up to, but she didn't have to think or come across it if she could really help it. She couldn't decide whether her mum was pulling her leg or not when she asked her if she knew that there was a 'naked gardening day' and if that was something Tom partook in!

It seemed that the magnetic pull of the house was pulling everyone closer together, strengthening family ties and holding friends and allies close, binding the past and the present together.

Chapter Seventeen

Rose was so pleased to get the house back to herself. She loved sharing it with Lisa, but her best friend was a real whirlwind and she found it a real effort keeping up with her. The first couple of days of Lisa's stay, after all the excitement of opening the mysterious box and finding the huge mirror in the attic space of the outbuilding, were spent chatting and catching up. Sharing good wine and good food, making stories up about the house and its previous occupants and enjoying each other's company again. They had both caught the sun and had a sun-kissed glow about them. Lisa had come downstairs for several days in the skimpiest of bikinis, enough to make any hot-blooded man blush. Her reason was to avoid tanning lines. So, Rose sat Lisa on the far side of the biggest shrub she could find, thankful that Tom had not cleared and tidied the whole garden and parts were still unkempt. Mickey was the only person who had found the pair of them that day and that was only because of Bert's exceptional spaniel nose, who had sniffed them out with no problem. Mickey was not going to forgo his daily slice of cake and chat just because the girls were hiding! Although, he did get an eyeful for his trouble.

The last part of Lisa's visit was all go. She wanted to get the front room sorted, tidied and cleaned. She was very disappointed when she realised that all the purchases for the new room were not going to arrive before she left. Rose, 'the voice of reason', kept telling her that the room was not finished and there was still loads to do, according to Steve, but she wouldn't listen. Lisa and Rose were at loggerheads for the first time since they were teenagers at school.

As Rose watched Lisa's car disappear up the lane from the end of the drive, she turned back towards the house. She grinned from ear to ear and retraced her steps towards the front door, mirroring her actions from the first time she ever set eyes on her inheritance – the house. She stood in the shade of the apple tree looking at the front door of her very first owned property, not rented. Her first home.

The house did not seem forlorn now. In terracotta pots by the front door were two box plants in a tall pyramidal shape. In front of those pots, stood smaller pots filled to the brim with all manner of summer bedding plants, spilling an array of colour onto the front step. There was barely room to swing the proverbial cat or indeed the cat of the house, Mowzer.

She reached into her pocket for the front door key and felt incredibly silly as she had come out of the back door to see her friend off, and the back door was propped open. She unlocked the front door and stepped into the hall. She looked up at the stained-glass windows running alongside the stairs, smiling at the colours that fell onto the bare wooden stairs from the nautical designs.

She did not retrace her steps through to the galley kitchen or into the back room and curl up on the window seat to enjoy her newfound peace and quiet. Astonishingly, she turned into the front room, walking across to the fireplace. She crouched and looked into the empty fireplace, seeking the Captain's hat that she had found with Lisa and Steve. The grate was clean and free from dust, although she had never ever swept it and to her knowledge neither had her friend. Rose was crushed as she wanted to trace the outline of the missing hat with her fingers. She wanted to remember.

She paced up and down the room, willing the house to remember with her. As she paced, she looked into the mirror still resting against the wall. She expected to see a pair of black boots pacing alongside her, marching with her. The only reflection she saw was her own. She made herself sigh once. Then twice on the second time, making it more dramatic. A big breathy sigh, still nothing. Nothing at all. The mysteries of the house could not be conjured at will. Frustrated, she kicked one of Lisa's boxes, for she didn't think of them as hers. It was all Lisa's ideas, not hers. It felt cathartic, so she kicked it again harder. Then heard a cough, a determined cough. Loud enough to get her immediate attention.

"I remember you doing a little dance in the back room when I first met you. Now you are kicking that box with an almost evil intent. You OK, Rose?"

Another sigh escaped from Rose as she turned to face Steve standing in the doorway, with his familiar wry grin plastered across his face, splitting it almost in two. His eyebrows were rendered lopsided by the grin and his eyes sparkled with humour.

"Oh, it's just you, Steve!" she said.

"Charming, Rose," Steve replied, his grin starting to fade. "Nice to see you too!"

She remembered her manners, but not before noticing that she had really hurt his feelings this time. "Steve, I am so sorry. I was just hoping you were going to be someone else."

"I know you must be missing Tom, by now, but there is no need to be so obvious, Rose." He avoided her eyes and looked at the floor instead.

"Oh, Steve, I am really so sorry, that is not what I meant at all." She grabbed his arm and pulled him into her and gave him a big hug, then released him with a shy smile. "I am so silly. I was willing 'something' to happen in here, but that's not how things work in this house, is it?"

Rose was talking about her ghostly companions and the Captain's hat, but Steve immediately misunderstood.

"You wanted 'something' to happen with me?"

Rose sighed hard, realising the implications of what she had just said.

As Rose and Steve stood facing each other, both feeling incredibly hot and uncomfortable and not knowing what to do or say, there was the sound of footsteps upstairs pacing across the floorboards. From left to right and back again, directly above their head.

"Rose, I didn't see Lisa's car by the house. I thought she had left, and you might want some company and to talk about this room without her constant suggestions, but she is still here. What have you done with her car? Where is it?"

Rose shook her head and held Steve's gaze in her own, as the pacing became more frantic, and the thudding started to beat through the house. Then, the pacing changed direction and the footsteps clattered down the stairs and stopped at the bottom.

Neither Steve nor Rose could see who was there without moving and neither of them made an attempt to move at first. Steve had his back to the door and Rose had to move slightly to the left in order to see. She reached for Steve's hand, shifted her weight onto her left foot and then leaned to the left, to peer around his torso and over his shoulder.

The hallway was empty, she could see that there was nobody there.

Meanwhile, Steve hadn't moved, he was glued to the spot staring at the footprints forming in the dust on the floorboards around Rose. The movement was silent and deliberate, so Rose was unaware that anything was happening and that the footprints had stopped right next to her shoulder.

Steve, blinked hard, for he couldn't see anyone there either.

Chapter Eighteen

The house grew silent once more, as Rose and Steve stood rooted to the spot for several minutes. Steve was transfixed by the footprints on the floor beside Rose. He was unwilling to move and was startled when Rose instinctively reached out to hold him. Rose was drawn to him, wanting to soothe his obvious discomfort, hug him tight and make his face crease into his familiar, lovable grin.

As she pulled him into her, she enveloped him in a big bear hug and rested her head on his shoulder. She looked up to see if her actions had made him smile and saw that his face was still set in the same expression. His eyes were still focused on a point behind her. She squeezed his shoulders gently before she pulled away and turned to look in the same direction, following his gaze and looking at the floorboards beside her.

She didn't see the footprints on the floor that Steve was looking at. She saw a faint outline of the familiar dainty black boots, the hem of a white dress and the pink ribbon trim. As her gaze rose to waist height the figure was barely visible and by the time she got to where her shoulders and head should be, there was nothing there. In the grate beyond sat the Captain's hat, as if it had always been there, and hadn't been missing at all.

With a delighted giggle Rose looked back at Steve. His bemused expression told her that he had caught a glimpse of her female companion. There was something else though, something odd happening with his face. She stared as his face changed, his features were altered slowly and ever so slightly. His nose, chin and hair became different. But his lips, pursed together in a wry smile, were the same, as his face slowly changed to that of the Captain.

Rose felt a compulsion that she could not resist even if she had wanted to. She licked her lips then stood on tiptoe and kissed him firmly on the lips. When his lips met hers, she leaned into him and pulled him close, as close as she could. As their bodies touched, the kiss intensified, their lips locked together as the passion grew.

It was Steve who broke away first, pulling away from her gently and walking backwards until he was in the doorway to the room. Rose watched him as he did so, befuddled and confused. She drew her arms across her chest and held her elbows tight. A solitary tear rolled down her cheek, when the features of the Captain started to vanish.

Steve stood motionless in the doorway, staring at Rose and her mirror image standing right next to her dressed in white with the tip of black boots just visible beneath the hem. They were almost identical, could be sisters but they were from different eras, different times, but the love that was radiating from both of them was pure and directed at him.

He shook his head from side to side at this incredulous notion, closing his eyes as he did so. When his head was still again and his eyes open once more, Rose was standing on her own in front of him. The feeling of love was diminished but still vibrant in the air.

Steve shook his head again and stammered an apology to Rose before he strode out of the house. He sat in his car for a while regaining his equilibrium and then drove home without a backward glance, leaving Rose alone in the house once more.

Chapter Nineteen

Rose and Steve avoided each other for the best part of a week after this peculiar set of events. They saw each other in the distance and waved politely, but neither of them wanted to transcend the huge chasm that had appeared in their friendship. Rose was still sure of her intense feelings for Tom. She was, however, unwilling to accept that she could have the same kind of feelings for two men at the same time. She kept telling herself she was not that kind of girl, and her feelings were just getting jumbled because Tom was away.

Whenever she felt herself pushing Steve away as she started to think about him, the air was filled with that heady fragrance once more and Steve's face was supplanted by the Captain's in her mind. The features of both the Captain and Steve were uncannily similar. The bright eyes, his cheeky grin and those endearing dimples in his cheeks when he smiled.

It seemed that more than one Captain had resided in the house and both men, Steve and Tom, resembled a different individual Captain. Or were the house and her mind playing tricks on her?

Steve wanted to confront Rose and her feelings for him, as he had always had a soft spot for her from the moment he first set eyes on her. The spooky 'other woman' had put him off, even though he knew that she wasn't a tangible threat in this lifetime. He was going to plan his next move with military precision, thus ensuring he achieved the right result. He didn't dare believe he could have a sliver of a chance against the 'big' romance that Rose had going with Tom and the whole garden vibe. He did, however, figure that he had a fighting chance; he was the 'big' man about the house. Rose's precious Captain's House. Tom was virtually useless with jobs in the house. He could design, plant and win awards for his gardens, but up against Steve for the equivalent task in the house, Tom would fail big time. Steve was going for 'gloves off' when it suited him. He carefully calculated that Tom wouldn't even see him coming. If Tom stayed away too long, would Rose be willing to take him back? Tom didn't even live there really, not yet anyway.

Steve continued to keep busy around the house and if he needed a decision, he texted Rose instead of popping over to discuss it with her over a cup of coffee. He kept his distance doing all the jobs that were furthest away from the main house and garden. His only contact with Rose was a cheery wave from afar and the workmanlike texts that were essential for the ongoing building renovations.

Occasionally, he thought that Rose had joined him and was standing near, but when he turned around there was nobody there, just a heady fragrance that lingered in the air. Other times he would hear a faint, breathy sigh in his ear which made all his senses tingle and immediately would think of Rose.

Then she was gone. It was after these moments that he would catch sight of Rose across the courtyard or sitting quietly in the garden in the sun. It was all he could do, to wave and smile at her as he realised that the fragrance and sighs did not belong to her, but the woman he glimpsed with Rose that afternoon in the front room when she looked at him with pure love.

Love was definitely in the air surrounding the house but Tom's text messages to Rose were getting shorter and shorter. More demanding with jobs for the garden. There was not a lot of emotion.

Rose was starting to feel like an employee of Tom's with a list of jobs for the day in her garden. Some of them were standard daily ones, like watering and deadheading. Others were detailed instructions about pruning a particular shrub or bush, accompanied by a photo or a hyperlink to a gardening website. It was as if Tom had forgotten the niceties of romance unless it was for his beloved garden. Rose was getting more disgruntled every time a message from Tom pinged up on her mobile.

Determined to prove to Tom that it was her garden and not his she decided to explore a bit more as the weather was set to fair for a few more days. She understood that Tom was renovating the garden area by area, but she wanted to find a piece of her garden to claim for her own again, even though the whole garden was hers anyway.

Fresh from a good night's sleep, she pulled on her gardening gloves and ignoring the fresh set of jobs that had just pinged up on her mobile, deliberately turned the opposite way and made her way to the pond and the brickwork that Lisa had told her about but not showed her.

As she crossed the garden, there on the exposed roots of the fallen beech tree sat two magpies watching her every step with their beady eyes and encouraging her in their imitable guttural croak. She smiled at 'her' black and white feathered companions and answered them with a, "Good morning, Maggie, and how is your lady wife today?" When they looked to their left she followed their gaze and was startled by what she saw. She wanted to blink hard a couple of times. Not wanting to risk it, she didn't. She continued to stare so hard it made her eyes water.

She couldn't quite believe what she was seeing.

Chapter Twenty

Rose continued to stare.

At the ghostly female presence that was so very familiar. Just a soft puff of breath on her cheek or neck, she was not in her usual place, right behind or beside her. But she was so sure that it was her ghostly companion she saw in front of her, perched on a mound of bricks in the far corner of the garden. Rose wasn't close enough to smell her heady fragrance so was a bit unsure if it was her or someone else; she was a little too far away to be certain. There was a menacing pall of smoke eddying around the figure which made her disappear sporadically as Rose continued to stare. The smoke swirls became thicker, and it was even harder for Rose to discern if anyone was really there. She slowly paced towards the figure that was beginning to fade into the greyness. She was uncertain if the woman was real or not as the shadows that were forming were not staying still but flickering in the sunlight, so when she was close enough to touch her, she extended her arms. Stretching her fingers wide and splaying them to their physical limitations. Her actions were in vain when the smoke made her cough and splutter. Her eyes started to water so she brought her now clenched hands to her eyes and rubbed them ferociously. She wanted to see, wanted to touch. She needed to make the presence a certainty, a fact. She needed to be sure. Her eyes were full of tears and rubbing them only made them worse.

Then suddenly she tripped and fell.

She landed in a sprawling heap and slumped sideways, making her head swim until she felt herself being carefully caressed and her head being supported by something warm and soft. A hand was stroking her hair then her cheek very gently with real affection. Bewildered, she opened her eyes and through the wetness of her tears saw the face of her companion as her head was resting in the lady's lap. The lacy cuffs of her dress were tickling her face. She closed her eyes and let herself just be. Comfortable and warm. Until her nostrils were assaulted by the acrid smoke once more, which sent automatic danger signals to her senses. She was loath to move but the smoke had silently encroached onto the space again, urgently enticing her to sit up to cough. She coughed as she pulled herself upright and gingerly moved over so she could sit next to her companion, right up as close as she could. She craved the intimacy. With an imperceptible nod, the lady sensed her urge and her arm snaked across Rose's shoulders and pulled her in tight, while her hand reached for Rose's, placing a handkerchief in her palm. Glancing sideways, Rose caught sight of an identical handkerchief in her hands. She was not coughing and spluttering like Rose. She was silently crying, dabbing her eyes with her free hand, as tears rolled down her cheeks, leaning in towards Rose, seeking a mutual comfort from her too.

The smoke enveloped them both, getting dense and thick. Rose caught her breath then panicked as she couldn't breathe. There was a faint ringing in her ears, a shrill warning that she was going to lose consciousness or pass out if she didn't get out of the smoke soon. She stumbled to her feet and managed to walk a little way before slumping once again to the grass and closing her eyes.

When she woke, the smoke was gone. The sky was clear, and the sun was shining. She was laid prone on the unkempt grass for all intents and purposes as if she was sunbathing. Her arms were behind her head, making a makeshift pillow and allowing her to look around without getting up. She was in the same spot where she first spotted her ghostly lady sat atop the bricks. It was as if she hadn't moved or approached her in anyway. Bitterly disappointed, Rose moved her arms from behind her head, wincing as they were numb. She brought her arms across her chest and rubbed them to get the blood flowing again. It was then that she noticed she was holding a handkerchief. Lacy and pure white, with tiny pink roses around the edge, matching the dress of her ghostly companion.

She held it to her nose, closed her eyes and breathed in the fragrance that she knew so well, until the tinge of smoke assailed her senses once again. Her eyes grew wide when she opened them and remembered.

Only the handkerchief she was holding was now a dull grey, the lace trim mottled with black smuts. No trace of the pink in the embroidered roses remained.

Chapter Twenty-One

Back on her feet but with the cloying smell of smoke clinging to her clothes and hair, Rose ventured to the boundaries of her garden seeking the source of the smoke. The farmer who used the marshland surrounding the cottage grazed sheep and was not one to light a bonfire. She had no close neighbours who would be lighting a fire, especially in the middle of the afternoon. The smoke worried her, and she clambered through the undergrowth of the hedge to make sure that there was nothing to be worried about. She followed the line of the hedge on her neighbour's side, noticing for the first time how much wood and other building rubble was scattered and dumped along the hedge line. It was barely noticeable until you were on top of it as the weeds and other foliage had hidden it from plain sight. She walked until she was level with her house but on the opposite side of the boundary line, until she came alongside the river on its way to the sea, on the other side of another copse of trees that formed an informal boundary differentiating her acreage from that of her neighbour. She stood on the riverbank and looked across at the folly and beyond to the sea.

There was no lingering smoke, and the still air just carried the scent of the sea. A salty tang. The shadows remained, they hung long and dark on the other side of the copse, the old house forming the shadow of a wall that wasn't there. Was this a part of the house that didn't exist in Rose's world, but the essence of it remained?

Oblivious to the shadows and reassured that there was no sign of fire, smoke or anything sinister, Rose tried to make her way through the tightly knit copse of slender trees back into her own garden, marvelling at the impermeable layer of vegetation akin to that of a tropical rainforest. The ivy was running rampant up the trunks from tree to tree, using every branch, large or small. She literally walked into a wire fence that was obviously there to stop any livestock coming into her garden. She expected it to give way to her body weight as it looked like a screen of ivy tendrils, not a fence, but it didn't. She stumbled into it at full pelt, crashing into the wire and coming to an abrupt stop. She then retraced her steps back to the riverbank and stood still to contemplate if she could manage to slide down the steep riverbank and paddle back into her garden barefoot through the water. With a giggle she sat down alongside the bank and slipped her trainers and socks off.

She was halfway down the precipitous bank when she was accosted by Bert, Mickey's lively spaniel, who had come to meet her from the other side of the river, where he was being walked along the footpath from the folly. With a loud splash, Rose slipped the last few feet down the bank and into the water. Bert thought this was part of the game and gambolled around her, jumping up and down and making her thoroughly wet. He then started to bark in delight at the sight of Rose in his favourite place – the water – for the first time, joining in his doggy games.

Luckily the water was not too deep where she landed and was just knee height, but that didn't stop Mickey running to the edge of the opposite riverbank to make sure Rose was all right.

"Oh, Mickey. What a day! Don't worry, I am all right. Just a tad wet, you know. Can you call Bert back to you, so I can stand up? I am starting to get a bit chilly. The water may look warm, but I can promise you it's not. It's very cool."

With a throaty chuckle, Mickey called back, "What are you doing over there? Why the slide down the bank from over there? What are you doing in Jimmy's field anyway? I would hurry up as the sheep are going for a gander and are coming your way too. Jimmy will be furious if you have shown them the way into the water. He likes them to stay in that field now and onto the marshy parts of his land later on in the year."

"How come you are so knowledgeable about Jimmy's sheep all of a sudden, Mickey?"

"Well, I met Jimmy that other day on my walk to the folly and we had a nice chat. Never really spoken to him before much, as he is not much of a drinker and never supped at 'The Ship'."

The banter flew back and forth between them as Rose waded through slightly deeper water, holding her trainers aloof with Bert splashing at her side. She wondered why she was expending more energy than she needed to in an attempt to keep her trainers dry, when they were already wet. Mickey just thought it was a 'women' thing as he kept a watchful eye on Rose and Bert from the opposite bank. When Mickey saw that she had reached a bit of the bank that was easy to climb on his side, he called down.

"Stop your adventures now, young lady, and get yourself up here on dry land and bring my wet dog with you, Rose!"

With a giggle and a smile, Rose climbed up the muddy bank to Mickey after the trainers she had already slung up to him, in a half-hearted attempt to silence his admonishment.

When she had retrieved her trainers, she glanced back to check that Bert was with her. He stood by her side with her discarded wet socks in his mouth, sporting what could only be described as his best doggy grin. She was sure that Bert totally agreed with her earlier comment of 'What a day!'

He dropped the socks at her feet along with a scrap of grey material. The pink hints of the embroidered flowers were long gone, replaced with the muddy green tint of the water from the river. The handkerchief was soiled and dirty. She snatched it away with an uncharacteristic yell of disgust aimed at Bert, who cowered from her in surprise. She stuffed it in her pocket and ran away from them both, in a huff, towards the house.

A dumfounded Mickey with Bert winding around his legs for comfort watched her go.

"How very odd, my boy. Let her go for now. We will follow her in a bit, to check she is OK as our Rose is out of sorts. Whatever was it with her socks that upset her so? Don't fret, my boy. Dad will sort it…" he mumbled gently at the dog at his feet, ruffling the fur on Bert's head as he did so.

Chapter Twenty-Two

Mickey arrived at the house with a very subdued dog at his feet after Rose's uncharacteristic outburst. He was greeted by all the doors of the house firmly locked, preventing him from just wandering in to check on Rose. When he walked around to the front of the house, he could just make out the shadow of Rose peeking out from the side of the front window.

He thought it was Rose but couldn't really be sure as she kept moving away from the window every time he peered in, cupping his hands around his eyes to keep the glare from the bright sunshine from the glass in the window.

Bert whined at his feet and continued to whimper until Mickey led him away from the house and towards the outbuildings and the little utility room where Rose housed most of her white kitchen appliances, as there wasn't enough room in the tiny galley kitchen of the main house. It was where he and his friends used to spend their afternoons when the main outbuilding was being renovated. There was still a kettle on the worktop, so Mickey rummaged around till he found a mug in one of the cupboards and a box of teabags and made himself a cuppa while he settled down to watch and keep an eye on Rose from a distance, through the utility room window. He could see the side of the house from there and the silhouette of the back. It would have to do, as Mickey was not going to return home until he was sure that Rose was alright.

Mickey sipped his tea as opposed to his normal noisy slurping. Between his dainty sips, he propped the bottom of his mug up on the windowsill. The room felt cool and a bit chilly after the warmth of the midday sun. Bert curled up on a discarded bath towel that was in the corner of the room in front of the washing machine. Mickey didn't know if it was clean or dirty but didn't have the heart to move Bert. He let him curl up, his nose resting on his back legs with his tail underneath him. The dog's breath steady and slow as he slept.

The silence was overwhelming and unexpected. The outbuilding was normally full of people coming and going every day of the week. It seemed that everyone else had somewhere else to be or that they all needed the quietness to concentrate on their work. The businesses that rented Rose's outbuildings were diverse, ranging from florists, printers, painters, distinguished caterers, with some new ones joining the fold in the last few weeks.

Mickey's buddy Dennis, a photographer, worked out of the smaller of the outbuildings, sharing with Steve and his friends in the building trade and Tom's flourishing garden business. Bert, his spaniel, loved the fact that Dennis worked close by, as his wife had an assistance dog. Hearing Dogs for Deaf People had partnered her with his sister, Bunty from their renowned 'B' litter. All his siblings had been given names starting with the letter 'B' and they had all gone on to help their lucky applicants cope with life and varying degrees of hearing loss. Some of the litter had gone on to be hearing dogs, like Bunty. Others were not accredited so unable to wear the uniform, but still assisted their owners around the home with hearing loss as a sound support dog, like Bert. The fact that Bert was sound asleep meant that Bunty was not in the vicinity, as Bert would have sought her out and would definitely not be dozing quietly.

Mickey approved of the new businesses that had recently acquired space from Rose. Laura, a very quiet girl, had set up a work bench, making exquisite and flamboyant jewellery with silver and other metal as well as precious stones. She also collected interesting pieces from the beach, weaving these into her designs. Harriet, another florist, worked alongside Tilly, sharing her workspace, work bench and other equipment but keeping their businesses separate, as Harriet worked with silk and dried flowers. Unlike Tilly who only worked with fresh flowers with a definite preference for local and seasonal. Together they constantly fascinated and teased everyone with their 'is it real or not?' challenges, comparing their formal flower arrangements and blousy bouquets. The shrieks of delight when others got it wrong reverberated around the big barn. Mickey often bore the brunt of their laughter as he always got it wrong and was never, ever right.

Mickey got on very well with Arthur, previously an antique dealer who had branched out into upcycling as a retirement plan after chatting with Bob and Doreen, the former owners of 'The Ship'. Doreen did not have the courage for another venture and poor old Bob, her long-suffering husband, did not have the finances to cover his wife's new business ideas. She persuaded her old friend, Arthur, to take the plunge instead. He couldn't settle in retirement and wanted to keep busy, so he pottered about happily looking for suitable items to upcycle and Doreen used her design skills to repurpose and reimagine his finds.

Arthur was working well with Doreen. A bit too well, Mickey thought, as Arthur was very familiar with Doreen, a bit overfamiliar for Mickey's reasoning! He wouldn't have wanted his late wife, Iris, working so closely with another man. Mickey realised that his views were old fashioned and very out of date these days. He was nearly hung, drawn and quartered by Rose, when he happened to mention in passing that he had liked his Iris at home when she was alive, looking after him and making him a hearty meal at the end of his working day that was hot when he got in. He reckoned that poor old Bob had to put up with a warmed up meal or one of those microwave meals, as Doreen was never home these days.

Rose hadn't known that Doreen was working with or for Arthur when she accepted Arthur's proposal for renting some business space. Rose was still slightly cautious about Doreen after the painting fiasco when she first moved in, when Doreen had got mixed up in her ex-boyfriend Mike's scheming. So, her carefully laid plans of only accepting people she liked to work in her properties, had fallen a bit short, when she realised that those people could employ who they liked, and she would have to put up with them working on her doorstep. The only flaw in her well thought-out business plans that she had deliberated on for months after moving in.

The silence continued, without the usual birdsong, the guttural croak of the magpies that had made the skies around the house their own, or the cooing of the wood pigeons in the tall oak trees at the footpath entrance. To Mickey's surprise the only movement he had seen since he had been sitting there quietly pondering was Mowzer, but he wasn't prowling in his usual manner. He was cowering in the shadows of the corner of the house, looking as forlorn as his mistress.

There was something most definitely not right, but Mickey was clueless for the moment. He was startled when the silence was broken, when Bert started to whimper in his sleep. After waking with a start, Bert stood waiting at the door, and broke the silence again with a loud bark filling the tiny room with the noise. He scraped at the door with both paws, anxious to get out.

Mickey toyed with the idea of letting him out at all. *Does he just need a wee?* he asked himself as his hand remained on the door handle without turning it. Tilting his body to the left to peer out of the window before turning the handle, he looked out to see what Bert was barking at.

Mowzer had not moved, he still cowered in the shade of the corner of the old house, his body completely still, for all intents and purposes a stone statue resembling a crouching cat. His eyes wide, watching. Bert continued to pound at the door with his paws in his desperation to get out.

Mickey opened the door a chink to look, and Bert pushed past him in his haste to get out. The spaniel ignored Mowzer and Mickey's yells of "Come back here!" dashing around the corner of the house as if he was chasing something.

Mickey stood in the driveway and scratched his head.

There was nothing there. Or was there?

Chapter Twenty-Three

Bert's disobedience was such a rare occurrence that Mickey was rooted to the spot with surprise. He continued to scratch his head in disbelief as he surveyed the scene. It was not in Mickey's nature to be impulsive. He always took a moment before doing or saying anything, so he stood still, stopped bellowing for Bert to 'come' and waited in the relative safety of the doorway, hidden behind the door.

He was not as well hidden as he thought for as soon as Bert dashed past Mowzer, the cat took the opportunity to sprint in the opposite direction and flew in through the open door and between Mickey's legs, and from there up onto the countertop. From there he jumped onto the windowsill, crouching low to hide.

All was silent, as Bert's shrill barks could no longer be heard. Mowzer's whiskers twitched along with his nose which was pressed hard against the windowpane. His eyes were wide and unblinking. He was staring into the distance.

Once Mickey had got over his initial shock that Bert had raced off and not come back when he called him, which was extremely rare, as well as worrying about his dog, he started to worry about Rose. He wondered if she was frightened and that was why the doors of the house were uncharacteristically locked and bolted in the middle of the day. The rational part of his brain concluded that she locked the doors as she was desperate for a shower or soak in the bathtub after her impromptu dunk in the river. He always maintained that a soak in the bath was an ideal way to calm down too, and his Rose was very het up about something.

Mickey wanted to find out and didn't want to appear overbearing or stalker like. His current actions could be taken that way and here he was, huddled behind the door in her utility room keeping watch on the house.

As he went to sit down, the familiar bulge and discomfort in his buttock reminded him that he had his phone in the back pocket of his trousers. Cursing himself for not thinking of it before, he stood up, retrieved his phone and dialled Rose's number.

The phone rang out and then went to her automated answer phone message. He tried again and on the third try, he got an answer.

"Mickey, are you checking up on me?" she answered without letting him speak.

"Of course I am, Rose. Are you sure you are all right?" he asked in the tone he usually reserved for children and animals.

"I have just got out of the shower and I am just rough drying my hair with a towel, which is why I didn't hear the phone right away, as I see I have a couple of missed calls from you. I am sorry I was a bit odd with you. I just needed to get in the house right away. I really don't know why. I just did." Rose felt the need to explain herself to Mickey as she caught the low, soothing tone in his voice that he had never really used with her before.

"Oh, Rose, I was just worried because you had locked all the doors behind you. I guessed you might have wanted a shower, so I totally get it."

There was a pause. Quite a lengthy pause before Rose whispered, "I didn't lock any doors behind me. I just legged it up the stairs. Not even sure if I shut the back door to be honest, it was pinned behind the door stop, to stop it banging in the wind."

Whispering even softer with a tremor in her tone, "Mickey, I didn't lock the doors. I know, I didn't. What am I going to do? I am in the front bedroom, but I can hear someone downstairs beneath me walking about. I didn't hear any noises before you called, but I wasn't really listening to be honest."

"Rose, don't you worry, I am in the utility room just across the way, so I will make my way over to the front and take a look in the window. You stay right there and don't move. I will call the police if I have to. Keep quiet, Rose. Leave it with me."

"Oh, Mickey, do be careful. What are you going to do with Bert?"

"Bert is just fine," Mickey lied, to keep Rose calm. "Stop talking and sit tight. If push comes to shove, lock yourself in the bathroom."

Mickey shuddered as he ended the call, as did Rose in the house.

Mickey was right after all, there was something wrong and he had to face it without his trusty sidekick, Bert, at his side. He would face anything for 'his' Rose, so with a couple of deep breaths while checking that no one was in sight, he left the sanctuary of the outbuilding and made his way across the yard to the front of the house, dodging down beneath the windows to keep himself hidden and trying hard not to step or brush against anything that would give him away.

Chapter Twenty-Four

Rose crept along the side of her bed trying not to make a sound that would betray her presence in the house. She was heading for the bathroom, the only room in the house that had a bolt that she could pull across and keep herself safe. It was just like Mickey to think of something like that. As she was only in her knickers and bra, she grabbed some clean clothes from the armchair to put on in the bathroom. Whatever happened, she didn't want to greet it in a state of undress.

When she pulled the bolt across, she sat down on the edge of the bath and looked at the bundle of clothing she had picked up in her arm. Two pairs of knickers, one sock, another bra, a baggy T-shirt that she used for bed and a frayed pair of tracksuit bottoms that she wore around the house. She stifled a giggle as she got dressed in this motley array of clothing and tossed the surplus onto the floor.

It was all quiet, when she glanced at her phone screen to see if Mickey had called again after checking the house from the front. There was nothing, no display at all. With a sigh she threw it at the floor, where fortunately it landed on the pile of discarded clothing and didn't make a sound. Inadvertently mirroring the actions of Mickey earlier peering around the utility room door at the yard, she peeked around the now unbolted bathroom door. Hearing nothing, she crept down the stairs, her hands deep in her pockets, thinking as she got halfway down the stairs that she was empty handed and should have picked up something, anything to defend herself with. There was something stuffed in her pocket. Pulling it out, she stared at her hand. *All I have to defend myself is this!* It looked like a discarded dirty tissue, but when she looked closer, it was the hanky that she swore was on the pile of wet, smelly, dirty clothes that were in the washing basket at the end of the bath. The hanky had been stuffed in her pocket as she marched back into the house. So why was the totally dry albeit grey handkerchief in her hands now?

Rose was on the stairs trying to work out how this got in the pocket of her freshly washed tracksuit bottoms, when Mickey peered into the front room through the window from the outside.

The windows were all steamed up and this obscured his view. So he ducked down and made his way underneath the windows to the opposite side, which looked a little bit clearer. Moisture was dripping down the inside of the window, obscuring most of his view in. He got to the other side of the window in time to see an arrow form in the condensation, as if someone was drawing in the wetness with their fingertip.

The arrow was pointing directly at him and the sound of heavy footsteps from within the room were making their way to him as well, when he saw Rose open the door and walk in. Although, he thought it was Rose, but he wasn't quite sure. He positioned himself for a better look, ignoring the threat of the arrow betraying his position, in his concern for Rose. He did shrink away from the window when he noticed that the arrow was changing from a transparent mark in a sea of moisture to a dull black colour.

The sound of the footsteps were too heavy to be Rose and there were too many for just one person. Mickey wished he could see more but as he couldn't, he reached for his mobile to call the police. If Rose was careless enough to brashly walk into a room of uninvited guests, he would have to be the sensible one. When Mickey had made the call, he fully intended to rap on the windowpane and divert attention away from Rose and make whoever it was take chase. He was going to head back up the drive and into the workshops and hope someone would be there to let him in or give him a hand to confront the intruders.

He dropped the phone without making the call, in surprise when the windows cleared and the moisture vanished as did the arrow. He could now see that it was not Rose that had entered the room, but someone who looked very much like her. Practically her twin, he surmised. She was wearing a beautiful white dress, trimmed with pink flowers but she was on her own. She continued to walk across the room talking intently to someone else. A man, he assumed by the echo of their boots. The voice that answered was a male voice, but Mickey could only see a woman. The male voice got closer to where Mickey was standing and then moved away as they strolled across the room from the doorway to the fireplace and mantle on the other side.

He watched as the lady opened a door to the right of the fireplace and walked through. It was then he noticed Rose following closely behind the lady. In her footsteps almost. Mickey saw that Rose was wrenching something in her hands as she walked as if she was wringing out a dish cloth. Then she brought her hands to her face which was drenched in tears and dabbed her wet eyes with the cloth. He caught a glimpse of a piece of the same fabric as the dress the lady was wearing in Rose's hands and did a double take. Then he closed his eyes and shook his head in disbelief. When he opened them again, Rose had vanished too.

Chapter Twenty-Five

Mickey banged on the window and continued to rap on the glass, yelling loudly, as his eyes frantically searched the room for Rose. All the banging and yelling was not having an effect as the room in front of him through the glass remained totally empty. He turned and slumped to the grass under the window and put his head in his hands. He gave up for all of a couple of seconds, before he leapt to his feet and strode to the front door.

He came to a halt and stared at the door which was hanging limply on the frame. It looked busted and was hanging on one hinge. As he stepped inside, there was a distinct smell of smoke. Checking the back of the house and the kitchen first and then the upstairs rooms, Mickey was certain that nothing was burning within. Going to the front door again, Mickey was satisfied that there was nothing on fire, but the smell lingered. Following his nose, quite literally, Mickey made his way into the front room to the window where the black arrow had been drawn on the glass. It had reappeared. The black smudge of the arrow from this side looked like someone had drawn it with a fingertip. The blackness looked like it had been dipped in ash from the fire. Mickey made his way to the fireplace and its surround. The grate was black, as was the chimney breast and one side of the wall. The other wall was clean, still resplendent with the green wallpaper Steve had uncovered weeks earlier that Rose loved and wanted to keep.

There was a solid wall where the doorway he had seen from outside had been a moment before. The door, which was open wide when Rose had followed the lady, did not exist and the wall was covered in soot. With a wail Mickey sunk to his knees and leant back into the window frame. The mirror resting against the wall opposite was as black as coal. He crossed the room on his hands and knees and wiped it with the back of his sleeve. The soot came away easily.

Completely baffled, he stared at his own reflection in the newly cleaned surface of the mirror, thinking that he had gone completely mad or he was having a weird dream and hoping that he would soon wake, tucked up and warm in his own bed.

He cried at the injustice of it all, "Where is that Captain of Rose's when you need him, eh? Or that blasted hat of his. My bloody dog has deserted me too and the invincible Mowzer cat. Where the devil would they all be? How many times has Rose told me that this house has friendly ghosts? You don't seem friendly to me, you know. I am taking Rose away from the lot of you, you rotten lot… What's with the busted door and the smoke? Where's the bloody fire?"

He would have continued to rant, but for the chime of a clock.

A clock was chiming the hour in a very calming, sedate fashion. Mickey listened hard. He knew Rose didn't have a clock that chimed. It sounded like a big, old grandfather clock, with a swinging pendulum and a big beating heart and a regular, audible tick and chime. He glanced back at the wall where the door had been. The chime seemed to be coming from that side of the room. He could see the faint outline of what was indeed a grandfather clock, solid and imposing in such a small space tucked away next to the fireplace. The clock face was black and grimy, the whole clock was very dirty, but a glimpse of its original condition was there underneath the grime.

"If it's not bells at Christmas, it's bloody chiming clocks. Oh, bloody hell."

Mickey loved clocks and his little cottage was full of them. Glancing back before he got up, the mirror was clear again, not crystal clear as it was an antique after all. No blackness, no soot. The only sooty thing was his dirty sleeve that he had used to wipe it.

Or it was before Bert scampered into the room and into his lap. He was so pleased to have found his master that he scrambled all over him. Bert was covered head to tail in soot, dirt and dust. After washing his master's face with his wet tongue, he stood up in his master's lap with his paws on Mickey's shoulders and shook his body hard.

Mickey laughed and playfully pushed Bert away, but he still ended up absolutely covered, as did the floor, walls and anything within reach of the shaking furry body and tail. Pulling Bert back to him, he held him tight and buried his face in his fur.

The clock chimed once more, striking out the hour, and then stopped as suddenly as it started and silence befell the house again.

There was no sign of the chiming clock when Mickey got up again to have a good look at the it, and the mirror did not reflect Mickey and Bert at his feet.

The room depicted in the reflection was furnished, cosy and bright with a fire burning brightly in the hearth and the grandfather clock sat next to it in its own little alcove. The door on the other side of the fireplace was open wide.

There was still no sign of Rose in reality or reflection.

Chapter Twenty-Six

"Oh, Rose, where are you? Where is the lovely girl, Bert? Can you find her?" Mickey implored his faithful dog. Bert, always up for a game with his master, put his nose firmly to the ground and started to sniff. He sniffed at the wall, where the door had been and followed a scent all the way out of the room to the hall.

Looking back at Mickey, Bert barked excitedly and ran to his side, nudging his leg with his nose in true hearing dog fashion, as if he was alerting his master to a sound. He tapped Mickey's thigh repeatedly with his nose, then his excitement ran away with him, making him jump up and paw his leg.

Shaking his head in disbelief that his spaniel had just gone to the door and back and no further, he sighed. He then decided to humour Bert and follow him out to the hallway.

There out of sight until Mickey walked out of the front room, Rose sat at the bottom of the stairway, about three steps up, holding a tatty grey handkerchief in her hands. She smiled broadly when she saw Mickey.

"I know, it was a false alarm, wasn't it? The room was empty, just my mind playing tricks on me, or my mischievous Captain making his presence known again, was it?"

"You weren't there a moment ago, my love. You weren't *there*. You were in *there*. You *were*. Then you *weren't*!" Mickey tried to make some sense of it all.

Rose stood up and put her arms around Mickey. She held him tight for a while and then whispered in his ear, "Let's talk about it over a cuppa and slice of Val's cake, silly!"

"You weren't there, my love. You weren't, not sure if tea will sort it. Perhaps I need something stronger… a drop of whiskey. What happened to the Christmas whiskey or has Tom drunk it all?" Mickey replied.

"You must be feeling better as you haven't turned the cake down yet. I need a cup of tea. Tea makes everything better, doesn't it? You sit down and I will put the kettle on " Rose waved in the direction of the cosy back room, but to her surprise, Mickey turned around, walked back into the front room and pulled out a chair that was tucked underneath the dining room table. Bert settled down in front of the mirror and put his head on his front paws for a quick nap. Rose was incredulous when Mowzer strolled in as well and settled on the front windowsill, stretching out on the warm ledge.

It was only then that Rose noticed the state of Bert. Cobwebs hanging from his ears and his white fur stained with grey and black smears. The brown accents over his ears and eyes were barely noticeable under all the dirt.

"He was dripping wet when I last saw him. Where has he been, Mickey? And you, look at your sleeve. It's black."

All thoughts of a cuppa forgotten, she came in and grabbed his sleeve. "It's totally black. Ergh, you smell, you both do," looking across at the dog. "You stink of smoke. It was smoke that started all this when I was in the garden, you know." Grabbing a chair, she sat down and shared how she ended up in the river with Bert. She couldn't explain her bad mood, except that she felt cross, so very cross and needed to retrieve the handkerchief from Bert and she was angry that it was so soiled and wet.

She couldn't explain why though. She didn't want to mention the lady with the dress that matched the handkerchief to Mickey, just yet.

She handed the handkerchief to Mickey to make amends as she was sure he knew she wasn't telling him everything. His face frowned when he remembered her temper and the earlier events in this very room when Rose had vanished. He needed to share this with her, but he didn't want her to fret, so he was keeping something from her too. She was safe, well and with no smudges and dirt from the smoke, unlike him and Bert. Leaving the handkerchief in his hands, Rose got up to make the cuppa, after denying his further entreaties for whiskey. She went to the kitchen, leaving Mickey alone in the room.

Once Rose had left the room, Mickey got up and started to pace up and down. He went to the window and there was no trace of the arrow, so he couldn't share it with Rose now anyway. The window was bone dry and the only thing on the window was black and white hair from Mowzer who was now sunbathing on the ledge. Walking to the fireplace, mantle and hearth, there were traces of past fires, but no black soot or staining. The walls on one side were bare brick and on the other side of the hearth was the green wallpaper that Rose was so fond of that she wanted it to be copied to go all around the room, as it had done in the past. Mickey stroked the wallpaper and ran his fingers up and down the wall from the top to the bottom. Then he knocked with his knuckles. The wall sounded hollow. Going back to the bare brick on the other side he knocked again. Surely, Steve didn't miss this. A hollow wall, a doorway. On this side of the house there was nothing on the other side but garden. The garden that Rose was exploring that very morning.

Mickey felt a breath on the back of his neck that made him shiver. Surely, Rose could not have crept up on him that fast and the tea wouldn't be brewed by now. A warm feeling embraced him from behind, like a hug but without the bodily pressure. The smell of garden roses, heavy with scent hit his senses and made him sneeze. This sudden movement broke the spell, and as the fragrance dissipated, a giggle lingered in the air.

Chapter Twenty-Seven

It was very odd that the two good friends decided not to share everything with each other over their cuppa. Mickey was old enough to be Rose's father and he looked upon her as the daughter he and his late wife wished for, but never had. He planned to have a chat with Steve and a little wander in the garden himself when he could get Rose busy with something else, so she didn't notice him poking about. Rose looked upon Mickey as another father figure. She loved her own dad dearly and felt very blessed to have another 'dad' to look after her. With her parents living further away, she appreciated Mickey's company and advice with most things.

Mickey shared her sense of humour, fun and a love of all things sweet, so most days he popped in on the way back from his walks with Bert and shared a slice of something nice with a warm beverage, or if the weather was warmer a cold glass of lemonade or fruit juice. She was not going to share all the spooky goings on with Mickey as she knew he chatted regularly with her dad, and she didn't want him to spill the beans. She had unwittingly scared her parents before when a local man, Trevor, had got under her skin, threatening her inheritance and new business. They had never got to the bottom of what her ex-boyfriend, Mike, had really been responsible for and whether he had been the owner of the black car that had been mysteriously damaged out in the lane, opposite the house.

Rose planned to chat with Steve later about the builder's rubble she had discovered on the neighbouring land that she believed was once part of her house. Or it could be the remnants of an old farm building that used to be on Jimmy's land. Steve would know, she was sure. Unbeknown to both of them, the two good friends were thinking alike, and it was ironic that they both wanted to speak to Steve.

Indeed, in the course of the afternoon, Steve got two messages from both Mickey and Rose, asking strange questions about the old house and in particular the front room. There was even an obscure question about Jimmy's land too. Steve had questions about the front room too. Rose and Lisa seemed fixated on the room, which was remarkable as it used to be Rose's least favourite place in the whole house. As he sunk his second pint of the day, he continued to dwell on the infamous Captains' House and how bizarre to get two messages about the same property on the same day from two people who were probably spending the time together.

He was enjoying one of his rare days off. He craved space from Rose's house for a bit. He surmised that things were getting intense there at the moment and he didn't want a black eye when Tom returned from his time away if he deemed that Steve had put a foot wrong. Steve couldn't understand why Tom would stay away so long in the summer months when his business was so hectic. He had got other gardeners to cover his regular jobs, but that was always a dicey move in case they moved in on the customers while you were away. It was getting on for four weeks now, a whole month almost. Rose had said nothing and was doing a fine job of keeping on top of her garden by herself without Tom's help. She looked like she was getting a feel for all things botanical as Steve noticed several herbs recently potted up on her kitchen window sill. There were new plants coming up alongside the front of the house that looked like young roses coming into bloom, with new foliage and buds forming. They weren't there when Tom left, so Rose must have planted them in his absence.

Licking the beer from his top lip with his tongue Steve grinned at the thought, his grin getting wider as he imagined the conversation that Tom would have with Rose. Would there be a resentment from Tom that Rose was finally claiming the garden for her own? But would Rose ever have real feelings for him, he thought as he stared into the dredges of his pint. As he tipped the glass from side to side in his hand to swirl the beer inside around in a circle, he came to the warming conclusion that Rose was developing a real soft spot for him and that was something good and somewhere to start. When another message pinged, with 'we need to talk' displayed his pulse raced as he thought it was from Rose, until he looked twice. The message was not from Rose, it was from Tom.

How the hell did Tom know what was going on? Steve reeled as he continued to stare at the phone. Why was everything connected with the house so spooky? Three messages in less than half an hour all about the house, all about Rose, on the very afternoon he was trying so hard to get away and not think about it. Draining his glass, Steve picked up his phone to call Tom back straight away. It sounded urgent. He figured something must be, as he couldn't understand Tom at all. He had everything that he could ever wish for – the woman, the house, the garden and the roses that he was so passionate about, and yet he continued to stay away, extending his holiday week on week. Steve was ready for Tom to ask him to look after his Rose. Of course he would look after Rose, that question didn't really need asking, but if Tom didn't get back soon, he would look after Rose, and not in the way that Tom wanted. Steve was sick of playing fair. He waited too long for Rose when he first met her, playing the slow game, and Tom stole her from him. Not this time, he vowed. Not this time.

He was blown away when he ended the call with Tom and found out the real reason why he was staying with his parents for a while. He was shocked to the very core, when Tom said that he had not said a word of this to Rose and wanted Steve to keep his secret. Steve had guessed right earlier that Tom wanted him to keep a brotherly eye on Rose. He wished Tom hadn't told him what was happening, he should have told her parents or Mickey surely. It was important though, very important, and Steve knew he had to keep his promise and not say a word of this conversation to anyone, least of all Rose.

He really wished he hadn't drained his glass as he badly needed a drink now. How was he going to keep this news to himself now Tom had thrown a spanner into his relationship with Rose? Rose was the most important thing here, so he would do what Tom requested for now. Just for now. As far as Steve was concerned, Tom needed to get his act together and fast. Time was precious, as was Rose.

Chapter Twenty-Eight

Tom called Rose the very same day but in the evening time just as it was getting dark. He knew that Rose would be sat on the old bench in the garden watching the night settle as the dusk fell, as was her habit and his too, when he was with her. If the weather was wet, she curled up on the window seat and looked across into the distance at the folly and the sea beyond. He loved to talk to her at this time and always timed his calls to correspond with her habits. He almost felt he could be sat by the side of her with the wonders of modern technologies. It helped him deal with the fact that he was not there beside her, but he knew he had to return soon and explain the reason for his extended holiday. He wanted to do that face to face and knew he was running out of time, before things got difficult.

As expected, Tom wanted to talk about the garden first and foremost and to learn about her day. It was no surprise that he did not want to talk about her day and made assumptions about it instead. Rose didn't want to talk about the garden, she wanted to talk about the house and how it made her feel. How things were different without him there and how much she was missing him. She wanted to keep her garden private, close to her again. It was her garden after all and his enthusiasm about the unique planting was beginning to rub off on her.

She didn't get the chance. Tom was hard work to talk to and the conversation kept grinding to a halt. Disappointed and hurt, Rose wandered around the garden not really listening to Tom just injecting with a 'huh' and 'oh yeah' when the conversation ebbed. Tom, realising that Rose wasn't paying attention to what he was saying brought the whole painful process to a halt and ended the call with a heartfelt, "I love you so much and miss you, my Rose. I will be back with you in just a few days, my love."

Before she had a chance to reply, she heard another voice answer for her, loud and clear, "I miss you too, my darling. Hurry home now."

Rose spun around looking for the owner of the voice, expecting to see the woman now so familiar to her, wearing the white dress with the pink ribbons and trimmings. The fragrance was the only sign of her and that was barely there. The voice was so strong and clear that Tom thought it was Rose answering him as he ended the call.

Thoroughly out of sorts by the conversation and the events of the day, Rose couldn't settle as she ambled around the garden, pottering about. So she went back to the house, grabbed a jumper as the evening air was getting chilly and set off for a walk. She crossed the yard and went up past the outbuildings and onto the footpath that led up towards the folly. The folly was a neglected, disused tower that was also part of her inheritance. It was reputed to be haunted by the same Captain that gave her house its name, but Rose knew that her house belonged to generations of seafaring Captains and their women, not just the one. It was the women that were making themselves known now, sharing their emotions and memories of the house with Rose. Women who lived alone at the house while their loved ones, the Captains, were out at sea.

Ahead of Rose another lady of the house walked too, heading for the same place to watch for her man, her Captain. Rose was walking in her footsteps and those of generations of women that lived in the house before her. Occasionally, Rose saw a white flash in front of her and as the darkness grew, she blindly followed the familiar path up and along to the folly building itself.

The folly rose up dark and imposing when she reached it. The air was damp with a mist that was rising up from the ground. Rose was pleased she had put her jumper on, but was cross that she had not picked up her denim jacket with the key to the folly in the pocket. She sat on the bench outside instead and looked across to the sea. Above her, another woman looked out to sea, with a lantern in her hand from the top of the folly.

Rose smiled as the light from the lantern spilled onto her, sitting directly below. She gazed into the night and felt at peace. Tom said he loved her, and he would be home soon. She didn't have much longer to wait.

Chapter Twenty-Nine

For the next few days Rose felt thoroughly mollycoddled by her close friends and didn't have a moment to herself. It seemed that the world and its wife wanted to spend some time with her or ask something or needed attention for something urgent. She craved solitude and peace and it seemed that someone was always at her door, her phone was always ringing or there was a message coming through.

She had Dotty to help her with the admin stuff for the leasing of the outbuildings and their studio space, but everyone came straight to her instead. She found herself taking in deliveries for the residents of the studios and Tom. The back of the yard was filling up fast with all manner of plants, trees and shrubs. Pots of every shape and size were adding to what was rapidly becoming a green border to her outbuildings and Rose was being run ragged having to water all the new plants that were being delivered daily, in the increasing summer heat.

It was not how she envisaged her business going. She thought the business would run itself and she would have Dotty dealing with the admin, which was all there was to do on a daily basis. However, reality was not like that. What once was a peaceful, tranquil garden and her quiet retreat, turned into a real hive of activity for the best part of the day. Cars came and went at all hours, as customers popped into the new businesses. Cars were parked right outside her back door, and she had to look both ways to safely cross her own driveway to use her utility room, which had seemed like a good idea to have across the yard when the place was just hers. However, it was proving a pain to have to make conversation when grabbing something out of the freezer to cook for dinner.

Rose was pleased that it was all going well and didn't really mind, but she didn't know how to deter the nosy parkers that were only coming to take a look at the infamous haunted house. The odd folk that hung about pointing cameras into all the shadows, the ghost hunters that trawled the internet for spooky places to visit.

Maybe it was time to set opening times and rules for everyone who used her yard and buildings, so that she had the place to herself once again. She was reluctant to do this without thinking it through. She was becoming decidedly antisocial if she was left alone and was perturbed that no one seemed to be letting her be. She had no time to think. Tom rang constantly in the evenings and rambled on for ages about nothing really and Steve hung about the property doing a similar thing but in person. He was chatting about nothing really, but was just there, under her feet. Rose felt that Tom and Steve had worked something out between them. It was all a bit odd.

Val popped in during the mornings on her 'way to the shops', but she had never shopped every day before and Mickey was always there for lunch or afternoon tea, making sure he had a slice of the freshly baked cake that Val had left earlier on. She had a constant shadow, but not her familiar ghostly companion who was undemanding. She was shattered from making conversation. It was exhausting.

Rose was becoming utterly disenchanted with her new lifestyle and was beginning to think that Tom had the right idea to get away for a bit. Perhaps she should do the same, just get away for a few nights and stay with her mum and dad. She needed someone to look after the place though, to take care of the garden, plants and keep an eye on the business premises. Steve could water everything and make sure the place was safe and secure in her absence. Mowzer loved him and just needed feeding twice a day and fresh water.

So, she did just that on the spur of the moment, which was so odd for Rose, who normally planned everything months in advance. She locked up, packed the car and drove away, only telling her friends when she had arrived at her parents'. Steve already had a spare key, as did Val and Mickey. She figured they would work it out between them, so she sent the same message to all of them.

Out of sorts and released from the binding constraints of the Captain's House that had been an all-encompassing part of her life for so long, she sat in her childhood bedroom in her parents' place, far from her beloved house and all she held dear.

Or so she thought. That night and every night she stayed away from her home, as she slept, she went back in her dreams to the house, to her Captain, to her lost love.

Chapter Thirty

The Captain's House hadn't been empty for more than a couple of days or so, since Rose had moved in and even then, people were always popping in as the house wasn't completely finished. There was always something to be started or finished by Steve and his friends. People usually popped in the house to feed Mowzer if Rose was going to be late or stayed away longer than one night, but not this time. Mickey had moved Mowzer's bowls to the utility room, which had a cat-sized cavity in the door, and he was feeding him there. There was no point opening up the house just to let Mowzer in and out. There was no cat flap in the property and although he was house trained, no one wanted to be responsible for an accident.

Interestingly, no one volunteered this time to check on the house. Val, Steve, Dotty and Mickey all assumed that someone else was doing that. No one wanted to go into the house on their own. Dotty steered pretty clear of the house, after hearing all the rumours, as she had never experienced anything sinister or ghostly and she really didn't want to either.

Steve and Mickey had their recent experiences of ghostly goings on and were unwilling to push their luck any further, especially with Rose away. Val was happy to keep an eye on the place from a distance and living 'next door', albeit a fair way away just down the lane, she was often passing and stopped at the bottom of the driveway.

Mowzer adopted the towel that Bert had used for his crafty nap after his impromptu playtime in the river with Rose. Mickey had added an extra layer, dropping a couple of old tea towels onto the heap, so it was soft and cosy. Mowzer was happy with his new abode and perched on the windowsill to watch the comings and goings during the day when he wasn't napping. Most people popped in with little titbits from their lunch and to make a fuss of him, so he had more attention than he used to get with Rose.

Steve was happy to leave the house alone while Rose wasn't there. He wanted an excuse to keep busy in the house when she was there, not when she wasn't, so he deliberately left the work on the front room unfinished.

Mickey pottered about in the garden with Steve during the day, watering and tending the plants that needed care.

"What is going on here with all these pots, Steve?" he wailed across at Steve with now empty watering cans in both hands.

"I have been at this for hours it seems. Do you know what Tom is playing at with all these? Do they belong to Rose now or is he just keeping them here?"

Steve grinned at Mickey who was at the outside water tap, refilling both watering cans and wiping his sweaty brow. "No clue, mate. I think it is sacrilege that he is away having a holiday or whatever and leaving all this for Rose to look after. I can see why she wanted a break! I know Tom means well, but he is getting on my nerves. He needs to get back here now. Although he would have a bloody shock if he came back to surprise her and found the place locked, barred and empty, with his plants all droopy and in desperate need of watering."

"You are so right, he would. Don't you think the house looks different without Rose in it? It looks almost forlorn and unloved, all spooky again. All the time, even in this weather." Mickey glanced up at the clear blue sky with not a cloud in sight.

"Yeah, too right. I am not tempted to go inside at all," Steve replied.

Mickey raised an eyebrow and sniggered. "That's because Rose isn't there, isn't it though? You have a sweet spot for her, don't you?" His good-natured teasing made Steve flustered, and he ran his fingers around the neckline of his T-shirt.

"Too hot for this conversation, Mickey. I really don't know what you are getting at! I fancy a beer, I snuck a couple in Rose's fridge, let's get one each and then take a stroll around the garden and house. Make sure it's not too lonely without Rose and all locked up like it should be."

Moments later, both men strolled across the drive into the garden and settled down in the garden chairs. Mickey propped his feet up on the edge of the garden table, as did Steve, and they surveyed the house from this angle and slurped their beer straight from the can. Bert crept under the table and curled around for a snooze.

Both men were happy in each other's company and didn't feel the need for any chat. They sat in companionable silence until Mickey heard the back door banging on the door jamb. A constant thud as it was caught in the breeze.

As he sat upright taking his feet from the table, glancing across at Steve, he noticed he had done the same.

They exchanged a glance. Steve grabbed the broom that was propped up against the side wall along with other gardening tools that had been left there instead of being put away. Mickey picked up the rake. Without a word, they marched together to the now swinging back door.

Steve, who watched lots of action movies, copied all the moves from the films, making a gesture with his hands for Mickey to go upstairs while he would look in the two downstairs rooms. Mickey chuckled quietly at Steve's antics, pretending to be the 'big guy'. They had both forgotten Bert who flew in between their legs and bounded into the house before they could grab a hold of his collar. Eyes wide, they waited, expecting some kind of trouble.

Bert scampered into the front room, with his claws scrabbling at the wooden floorboards for purchase as he rounded the corner. The sound of which echoed in the empty hallway. The door was half open when he approached but Bert's bulk and impulsion forced the door wide with a clatter as it hit the wall.

After hitting the wall, the door rebounded and slammed shut before Mickey could get there. It was stuck fast. Mickey put his shoulder to the door in an effort to get it open but couldn't get it to budge even an inch. Steve came up behind Mickey. With a not so gentle shove, he pushed him out of the way and heaved his bulk at the door too. The door shifted in the frame but didn't budge much.

"Bert, you little monster, what have you done?" Mickey yelled at his dog in frustration. "You OK, Bert? Bert? Bert?"

Steve continued to push the door but he only succeeded in rattling it in the frame. He then stood back and aimed a hefty kick at the door handle.

"Mind Bert, you!" wailed Mickey. "He could be right on the other side."

The kick had the desired effect, and the door flew open wide. Steve stepped into the room and caught it before it could slam shut again.

Mickey stumbled into the room after him. They both stared. The room was completely empty. Where was Bert?

Chapter Thirty-One

Steve grabbed Mickey's shoulder to reassure him and looked under the table in the corner, expecting Bert to be there. He could see Bert hiding under the table in the reflection of the mirror that was still propped up against the wall.

"Mate, he is just here. Under the table." Taking his eyes off the reflection Steve bent down to find that the space under the table was empty. Just a few empty boxes.

"Oh what!" he cried as he stood up straight again.

Mickey was standing in the middle of the room, totally crestfallen. How could he lose his Bert again and in this creepy room of all places? He marched across to the wall and rained a volley of blows on it.

"Mickey, that sounds hollow, let me see," Steve whispered.

Steve examined the wall and started to pull away the loose plaster, until Mickey yelled, "Wait, Steve, listen."

Very faintly a clock chimed the hour. In that pause, Mickey heard a familiar bark from the other side of the wall. He raced out of house and Steve saw him dash past the window.

He listened as the clock continued to chime the hour and grinned as he heard the sounds of the dog and master reuniting in the garden. Going to the window he checked that they were fastened tight, but surely Bert must have jumped out of an open window. They must have startled an intruder who left in a hurry. Or did they? Even if the window was shut, the iron openings were still in their grooves, but if they were slammed shut, they would fall into the groove naturally surely. Or would they?

Unsure and uncertain, he went back to the wall where the loose plaster was flaking. Most of it was coming away from the wall. It was not as bad as that the last time he was in the room. Steve met Mickey at the front door on his way to his van to get some tools so they could prise it away from the wall for good.

"I'll check the house properly this time," Mickey said, picking up the discarded rake from the hallway. He trailed through the house, going into every room and checking that nothing was disturbed. Going upstairs and into the back bedroom, he gazed across the river to the folly in the distance and the footpath that he walked daily with Bert. There was no one about. He could see the birds flying around the folly, circling in the thermals above the building. The pair of magpies that seemed to congregate around the house were conspicuously absent. He idled by the telescope that was set up in this room and ran his hand over the end where he stood. Impulsively he looked through the glass and tried to focus on a point in the distance. It was blurred and despite his fumbled attempts to focus, the distance remained unclear. He raised the telescope and moved the alignment to the folly. Was that a woman sat on the bench? It was exactly where his Iris used to sit. His heart lurched and raced. He fiddled with the telescope some more and it looked as if someone had joined her. His heart sunk. It was not his Iris after all. She looked familiar, the woman. Was it Rose? Perhaps she was back, but who was that with her? A man…. Too much fiddling with the antiquated telescope brought his snooping to an abrupt end when his focus turned pure black. When he managed to clear it, the woman had gone. He caught the back of her as she rounded the folly towards the door, her white dress flowing behind her in the wind.

By the time Mickey returned Steve was staring at the plaster with Bert watching him from under the table.

"Is everything OK in the house, Mickey?"

"Yes, all good," he lied, "but what happened here? Where did Bert go? How did he get out?"

Steve pointed across to the window. "I reckon it was open and Bert legged it outside or was following a scent, but you look scared and like you don't believe me."

Mickey didn't answer, he just frowned and nodded his head in the direction of the wall.

Mickey and Steve surveyed the wall before they started to knock the plaster from it. The prized green wallpaper was hanging on by a thread. Steve handed Mickey a mask. The green stuff was poisonous, he had read somewhere, so he was taking no chances. He was pleased that Bert was hiding under the table on the other side of room, well out of the way.

It didn't take them long as the plaster was brittle in some places and strangely damp in others. Steve managed to take one piece out with the wallpaper intact so he laid it on the table thinking that Rose could keep that piece and frame it. Maybe give it to Lisa, as she was the arty one. Her mum and dad were in the art world and would know how to preserve it correctly. There was an odd covering under the plaster which seemed to be mortar based, and much tougher. They chipped and hammered a small area that was waist height and found a small hole surrounded by metal. As they uncovered more of the metal, they began to see what was underneath.

Steve whistled and drew back to have a good look to be sure of what he was seeing. Mickey didn't need to step back, he knew it was the lock plate of the door that he had seen wide open before.

The door that went nowhere, as the wall was complete on the other side with no clue that a doorway ever existed. How did Bert get on the other side? Who and what was he following? In this time or another time?

Chapter Thirty-Two

By the time dusk set in the men had uncovered all of the spectacular oak door that had been hidden for over a century. Also revealing an ornate stone mantel, which was out of keeping with the current house. Steve was exclaiming his delight with every chip of his chisel. By contrast, Mickey was abnormally quiet, working twice as hard next to him. Bert lay exhausted from his adventures under the table until they finished then he plodded over to investigate.

He pushed Steve aside with his body weight and sat next to his master, looking up at him with hopeful eyes, begging him to open the door. When this didn't work, he attempted to scratch it, as he wanted to go out. He was insistent that he wanted to go out of the old oak door, nothing else would do. Mickey pointed to the other door and walked with him out to the garden. He looked across the front garden to the upended beech tree that had toppled some months before, he was not going to look back into the front room as he was terrified of that strange door. The door that led nowhere, but everywhere and gave the impression that it sucked all he cared for in…

Mickey watched as Bert 'watered' the grass and then ran back to greet Steve coming up behind him. He continued to stare as Bert led Steve around the house to the other side of the newly exposed door in the front room. Mickey followed a short while later, still unsettled and not liking the idea of the door actually existing. Bert was pawing at the bricks that made up the external wall for he knew precisely where the door was on the other side.

Steve was peering at the side of the house, pacing up and down. The wall was nothing out of the ordinary, he already knew that as he had walked the length of the house many times before with and without Rose. There was no sign of a doorway, the brickwork was complete and ran top to bottom, hiding any extra visual clues. He had compiled a comprehensive quote when renovating the house for Rose and he was cross that he had missed the concealed door. He was surprised that Rose had too. She had read too many mystery and adventure books as a child and was always tapping on surfaces looking for hidden compartments and finding carvings in obscure places, and coming up with absurd theories as to why they were there.

Steve knew how she missed the door though, as Rose had never quite taken to the front room, even having to be cajoled into using it at Christmas. It was her only big dining room table to seat the family around, but she had resisted the suggestion till the very last minute. She preferred the eccentric notion of maybe setting up in the outbuildings with electric fires to warm the huge space, instead of lighting a fire in her own front room and using the dining table that was already there. Lisa loved the room and was dying to use her design and artistic flair to make it cosy for Rose, but Rose blocked her every which way. Steve thought it was very odd, that the old door was in that room and extremely odd that Rose didn't have a clue it was there, or did she and she hadn't told him?

He felt a little queasy in the room ever since he had seen the lady behind Rose. Why was there a clock ticking in the room periodically too? As far as he knew Rose was a modern woman who wore a watch and kept time using her mobile phone. There was nothing in the house with a tick.

Was the old house marking time once more, not with bells this time but with a clock? Passing time or recounting time. He wasn't sure. He was certain there was not a ticking or chiming clock in the house, but he would have a look next time he was there on his own. He was only going back to the house to lock up. Mickey looked decidedly unwell, so he was going to run him and Bert home in his van.

"Enough excitement for one day, you two," he said, propelling Mickey and Bert in the right direction. "Go grab your beer that we left on the table, here's my keys, open my van up and wait for me. I will lock the house up and be right there." Mickey didn't answer but a grateful grin appeared on his face.

When Steve got to his van he found Mickey and Bert sat in the front seat, Bert on Mickey's lap only too ready to go home. As he drove away, the last of the daylight fell away and the house was in darkness.

It remained in darkness until the light from the van's headlights could no longer be seen and the blackness deepened around the house. Then, one by one a light appeared in every room. A warm cosy glow from a lantern on every windowsill. A faint almost imperceptible light was just visible alongside the house and then flickering in the darkness the shape of a much larger house. Windows in the larger house appeared as more lamplight glowed from its windows. In the lower window of this bigger house next to the existing Captain's house, a silhouette of a cat looked out, its eyes shining bright in the moonlight.

Chapter Thirty-Three

The cat in the window wasn't Mowzer as he could be seen in the shadows stalking a mouse around the corner of the outbuilding, watched by a solitary owl waiting for their chance to swoop down and grab Mowzer's prey from under his nose. The owl was perched on the corner of the gable end of the outbuilding, adding an element of grandeur, looking to all intents and purposes as a carved stone gable end in the manner of a very elegant gargoyle.

The main house did not need any elements of grandeur for there in the darkness the lamps within made the shape of the original visible once again. The house had doubled in size. The current front door was dwarfed by the main front door which could be seen where the remaining cottage-sized frontage ended. The concealed door in the front room of the cottage led into what used to be the original hallway.

If anyone had been walking along the lane they would have seen the original house in all its splendour with lights blazing from every window. The straight path through the garden that Tom had found when he started to restore it, led through the hedge marking another entrance, which had been hidden by time and the hedgerow that had grown up around it. The hedgerow where Rose had found the 'Captain's House' signage that gave the house its name. What remained was cottage sized, although still a house. 'The Captain's House' title belonged to this bigger house, with two almost matching wings. The outbuildings grew in the darkness to match the house. The courtyard was cobbled and the soft sounds of horses whickering to each other drifted from the stables. From windows of the folly far away in the distance, there was an almost imperceptible twinkle of the lamps lit within the tower. Atop the tower, there was a metal framework housing a flaming beacon that could be seen from miles around and right out into sea. The cat in the window was not solitary for long, as shapes and shadows formed in the windows. Just above the whisper of the wind, murmurs of voices could be heard too and the tinkle of music, the notes lingering on the air.

The presence of the building grew stronger and the darkness faded as the strength of the vision increased. The shadows took the form of people with distinct faces. The diction in the voices became more apparent as they grew lounder with the characteristic Kentish accent becoming clear. As the darkness faded the colours grew stronger. The garden took on some vibrancy too as the light intensified. The white of the blooming roses visible first, then the green of the lawn surrounded by box edging and well-tended shrubs. The old apple tree was becoming a young tree again, slim of trunk and growing straight and true, not the gnarled tree that Rose had sheltered from the rain when she first saw the house. Indeed, Rose wouldn't have recognised the house now. The house was back to how it used to be.

Mowzer crept around the house from the outbuildings after losing his snack to the owl when he had momentarily lost his focus after finding a couple of discarded Prawn Cocktail crisps dropped by Dotty earlier that day, near the main outbuilding door. The owl had flown off to the oak tree to digest the ill-fated mouse. He prowled under the front window of the house and along the longer length of the building. Completely unfazed by the footprint of the larger house, the noise and the chatter from within, he made his way to the apple tree and paused as if he was waiting for someone. As he rested on his haunches, he raised his paws and continued to have a wash, not minding the wait. He lifted his head to greet them when they arrived and wound his little body around their legs purring loudly with delight. He then followed them to the bench and jumped on their lap, tucking his paws underneath him as he continued to purr.

The lights vanished one by one, until the house was in darkness once more and the colours faded into black.

Punctuating the quietness was the contended purring coming from Mowzer as he snuggled deeper into a warm, cosy lap.

Chapter Thirty-Four

Rose had stayed away from the house for the best part of the week. She was enjoying being home with her parents and having her every need tended to. Her mum was her new shadow, never far from her, constantly putting the kettle on to make her a brew. They were both worried that Rose had left her new home empty and was leaving it to her friends to look after it and her new garden. The previous summer Rose had never visited them, they had to visit her. It was an absolute pleasure as the garden was stunning. Tom was creating a masterpiece. Tom hated this comment, he was recreating the masterpiece that was already there. Bringing the original garden back to life, finding and encouraging the plants that were already there.

Pete, Rose's dad, was really impressed with his dedication to the garden, but wished he had the same passion for Rose on a daily basis. Tom seemed to take Rose for granted, as many men did with their women. Pete had learnt from many years of marriage to Joan, Rose's mum, that you had to care for and nurture the women in your life and in doing so, they did the same to you tenfold. He hated the notion that Rose could be staying away from her new home because she felt unloved and uncared for, due to Tom's many absences and his recent extended holiday with his parents. With the risk of interfering, Pete had secretly rung Tom, on the pretence of wanting some gardening advice for their failing camellia. While he had Tom on the 'hook' he asked him whether his parents were ill and was that why he was still there? Tom had been quick to answer, stating that everyone including himself was completely fine, he just had some business close by that was taking its time to complete.

It seemed a legitimate answer, but on speaking with Rose it turned out that he hadn't alluded to anything so specific when he spoke to her. It was a sorry state of affairs and Pete thought there was something he was missing. He worried that his daughter was home with them again, like a teenager coming home early from a night out with no reason. Rose fully admitted that she had everything she needed in her new home and her new business was doing well too. Joan and Pete thought the dilemma that had brought her home was easily solvable.

If the hubbub of the businesses that leased the premises was annoying Rose, she should set some opening times, or times when the premises were closed for use. Rose had people coming and going at all hours at the moment, as she wanted them to be able to work when they chose. She knew that creative people sometimes kept odd hours. It didn't seem to be the business activities that were bothering Rose, but the customers using their visits to the outbuilding premises as an excuse to look over the hedge or wander uninvited into her garden. She even had a family picnicking on her front lawn one Sunday afternoon, claiming that as they had visited Laura and purchased some of her jewellery they were entitled to sit down and have their lunch on the premises too. Rose had shooed them away. When she told Laura after they had gone, Laura was shocked that people could be so brazen and horrified that they had waved her jewellery in her customised paper bag in Rose's face, even producing her invoice as proof of their entitlement to stay.

Pete had spent all afternoon in his shed and knocked together several wooden signs for Rose to hang around the place. He even had some signs on wooden posts so Rose could knock them into the grass. The signs were marked 'Private' and 'No Entry'. He made a couple for Tom to put up the drive to stop people parking on the grass verges or next to a particular shrub, so close that they bashed and crushed the plants with their car doors as they got out. He even found a discarded chain and a length of twine that he thought Rose could string across the footpath at the end of the courtyard with a 'Private' sign to swing in the middle, which she could attach to the two oak trees. Or she could string them across the river to stop the indulgent parents letting their toddlers paddle in the shallow waters in the heat of the summe. The Captain's House properties were not and would never be a 'day out' venue on the way to the beach. He had several conversations with Rose about whether her new business should be a B and B premises like Val's and converting the outbuildings accordingly, or a farm/coffee shop using her gardens as part of the seating space.

Rose had hated the idea of all the people, all the time getting under her feet. She wanted to keep the house and gardens as her space. Letting the outbuildings to local businesspeople to use as a workspace was a good compromise. The success of her new venture and the stunning location, meant that the businesses were using it as retail space as well, inviting people over to take a look before purchasing or to collect their goods if they were local.

Why had she sought refuge at her childhood home once more? Was the hustle and bustle just an excuse? Her parents feared that it was, and that Rose was falling out of love with her new home or was she falling out of love with Tom, whose love of the garden had made him a firm fixture in her life and home.

Chapter Thirty-Five

Rose was thrilled with her new wooden signs that her dad had made, and was so pleased that she had her mum and dad to talk to. She enjoyed her days with her parents getting away from it all, but in her dreams, she never left her Captain's House.

Every night when she closed her eyes she was transported to the garden of the house, to stand under the gnarled apple tree, and she watched as the lamps appeared in every window and saw the shadows of those within. She saw Mowzer moving along the windowsills, keeping guard on the house, unaware that he was sleeping in his new bed in the utility room in the outbuilding and didn't have free access to the house at night-time.

She watched as men tended the garden in the moonlight, several of them wearing flat caps over their closely cropped hair. Occasionally she watched as the women collected flowers from the garden to display in the house. These women were not familiar to her, for they wore a uniform and looked like they were in service. The ladies of the house were too far away for her to recognise, as they looked out and met her gaze from the window. The ladies were never together. One upstairs and one downstairs, looking oblivious to each other's presence.

This scene played out night after night in her dreams while she was away from the house. Identical dream patterns. The lamps in the windows looked incredulous during the day, but the gardening scenes perfectly matched to the daylight hours and the following night the lamps in the windows and the women looking out into the darkness suited the moonlit setting, but the men shouldn't have been working in the garden by the light of the moon.

It was as if everything connected to the house was jumbled up in her head and in her dreams at night too. Until she went to bed a little earlier one night, so she was asleep for longer, when the dream played perfectly, as if the director of a movie had changed the lighting and rewritten the screenplay. The women of the house looked out into the moonlight but moved about freely within, their movement causing the candles within the lamps to flicker and shadows to play on the lawn below. The house shimmered and moved in the shadows until the house emerged from the darkness, in its entirety once more. The front door in the centre with two solid wings of the property on either side, lamps blazing from every window.

In her dream Rose sat on the bench in the garden and felt at one with the house, garden and its ghosts once more, part of the tapestry of the house again. She absentmindedly stroked Mowzer who had settled in her lap and gazed as her house transformed into its past glory. Rose watched as the women of the house came to the front door and stood arm in arm watching her. With a wave they beckoned her over to join them. She waved acknowledgement and went to push Mowzer from her lap.

"Only me, my love," said a familiar voice in her ear, as her mum roused her from her slumbers instead. Brushing her hair from her eyes with her hands she cried, "Oh, Mum, I have got to go home, today. My house is not what I thought it was, or was it a dream? Oh, Mum, I can't quite remember…"

It didn't take Rose long to pack and say her goodbyes. Her mum had wanted to go with her, but Rose didn't want company and she urged her mum not to worry. She assured her that she would call her when she got home safe and sound. Her dad was harder to convince that she was going home because she wanted to and not because of some silly dream that she couldn't really remember. Rose was sure on both counts, she knew the real reason that she had raced home to her parents was because she was fretting about Tom, about the future with him. The new busyness around her home was just an excuse as she didn't want to talk about her relationship with Tom, with her parents. She didn't know the answers. She knew she loved Tom with every fibre of her being and that they were meant to be together, but she also had deep affection for Steve and knew it could develop very easily and quickly into more. She needed to put on her 'big girl pants' and deal with it.

She was nearly at the house when she pulled over onto a layby to call Tom. She got his answering service every time. He was not picking up. She left a message urging him to call, to come home, to come back to her, and then just before hanging up, she sarcastically added 'and come back for your garden'. She regretted the last comment when she hung up, but left it hanging, not wanting the rigmarole of making another call and leaving another message.

Where was Tom and why was he not answering her calls? Perhaps he was working, she surmised, but on mulling it over, she expected him to call back. She deliberately set her phone to silent before she pulled out of the layby to finish the last little bit of her journey. He would have to wait for her now.

Chapter Thirty-Six

There was no one working in the outbuildings when Rose drove back up the drive. It was a Sunday, so it was always relatively quiet. Rose wanted people to work when the mood took them, so sometimes there was the odd person milling around, working on a special project or to a tight deadline on a commission. That was why she didn't stipulate any working hours on the original agreements. Perhaps the general excitement of the new business premises in the locality and the presence of genuine crafts, people creating and working there was wearing off. Rose certainly hoped so and on the busier days she would use the thoughtful gifts that her dad had made for her. The 'private', 'no access', 'no entry' and 'keep off the grass' signs.

Rose was still in a quandary about what had made her leave in a hurry. Was it the buildings, people, business or just her love life with her missing man and her faithful best friend that just happened to be male, single and very available when she needed him, causing her to stress?

She didn't unpack the car straight away even though she had perishable food that should have been packed into a cold fridge or freezer. A car full of goodies that her mum had packed, as she did, knowing full well that Rose did not live miles away from a supermarket, just in the country. A bit countrified, her mum called it, not like living in a town. She packed as if Rose was travelling back and lived in a wild, desolate place, not to the leafy green county of Kent.

Rose strolled into the garden, smiling broadly as she walked amongst the roses again, lifting individual blooms to smell their unique scent, marvelling at their colours and at the neatness of the garden all around her. The lawn was very neat, too neat and too short. The edges were sharp around the gravelled paths and when she cast her eyes up and towards the house she realised why.

The house from her dreams of the past few nights, was there in front of her in broad daylight, not the darkness. She strode up the main path that now had a purpose, as it led to a front door. It puzzled Tom that it was a path to nowhere when he was restoring the garden and had him scrabbling around in the dirt, looking for clues. That was when he had found a beautiful gold ring. Rose was very fond of the ring and wore it all the time. It was identical to the ring that was carved on the figurehead. It belonged to the house.

The two ladies were standing in the doorway to welcome her into the house. Rose hurried along, wanting to get there to greet them. They stood aside when she stepped inside and waved her across and into the room on their right. She slowed as she stepped in, taking in the grand staircase behind them with a round table in the large and rather grand hallway. On the table stood a large vase of roses picked fresh from the garden. She picked one as she passed, it was an unusual colour, she didn't think the ladies would mind.

As she passed through the doorway, she realised she was alone again, no one had followed her, for they couldn't as the door was firmly shut behind her. Rose didn't hear it close. She looked around and marvelled at the wallpaper with the familiar green design, the mirror that hung over the mantel and the dining table in the centre of the room standing on an expensive carpet on the floor. To one side of the fireplace there was a grandfather clock with a delicate clockface and exquisite painting on either side of the hands. The clock's tick marked the passage of time.

She stared as the hands spun around the clockface too fast for the steady tick that was coming from within. When they marked the hour, the clock chimed.

Time altered till she was standing in the empty front room of her house, the clock was no longer there, nor was the splendour. The mirror was on the floor propped up against the wall where Lisa had left it. She turned in horror at the faded oak door, still bearing remnants of the plaster that had covered it before Mickey and Steve had knocked most of it away.

The door was shut tight, but she could hear the ladies calling her name from the other side, until the clock fell silent as the chiming of the hour ceased. She lifted her hand to pound on the door, to let them know she was still there, there was no door handle to turn. She knew it was a fruitless exercise and as the voices faded, she expected the rose in her hands to fade too. It didn't, the flower remained as it was when she plucked it from the vase in the hallway of the big house. She rushed out of the room and through her front door to the side of the house, where the vase of roses had been on the round table in the hallway, to find a new rose bush. It was well established as if it had been there for ever. The rose in her hand was the very same colour. How had she missed this? The scent was intriguing and familiar.

"Ah yes, it's you. Your scent," she whispered as she felt a presence at her side once more.

Chapter Thirty-Seven

Rose was still standing there ever so slightly bemused and entirely in awe of the presence of the larger house. She could now recall the last of her dreams in detail. If she listened hard, she could still hear the voices of the women calling her name, but their voices were getting softer and softer until they were gone.

A larger house. How had that been forgotten in the locals' memory, in the archives? The Captains were remembered fondly, still talked about and still remained on everyone's lips, living on as ghostly forms by all who regarded the old house and folly as haunted. The door in the front room had been hidden from view, but she knew she had entered the larger house before. She was at a loss to remember where she had ventured and with whom. Had she been dreaming or was it a memory forgotten? Or were her memories becoming entwined with those of the women who had lived in the house?

Was that why she had been unwilling to touch anything in the front of the house, or did she know about the door and where it led? Would the house feel different now she knew, now the door was uncovered? The door that led to nowhere in the present but everywhere in the past.

She played with the rose in her hands and felt in the pockets of her jacket for the pruning tool that Tom had gifted her for Christmas. He had found it in one of her outbuildings and fitted a new handle and sharpened the blade. Laura had dabbled in leatherwork to create a cover to keep the blade safe in a pocket. After working on Rose's gift from Tom, she was contemplating, adding leather necklaces and bracelets to her jewellery range, instead of using the traditional gold and silver linked chains for her work.

Rose loved the thoughtful gift. She was pleased it belonged to the house and delighted that Tom trusted her to work in the garden. Even though it was her garden, she left it to Tom to prune all the plants. She never quite knew what to do and would have hated to mess it up and have to wait years for it all to grow back again. This spring and summer, Tom had been patient with her and she was learning how to manage the garden. To her surprise she enjoyed the garden jobs as much as Tom, if not more. It was work to Tom, but pleasure for her. She loved the way that Tom smiled at her, his eyes twinkling with delight as she learnt the rudimentary ways of pruning his beloved roses.

She took enough roses from the bush to recreate the display that had been on the round table and unlocked the back door to find a vase. She had seen a vase just like the one that was on the table at the back of the pantry with all the other forgotten crockery, porcelain and glassware. The kitchen was tiny, but the pantry was huge and went back a very long way. She only used the front bit as it was all she could reach. After moving all her tinned foods, biscuits and cake tins from the middle shelf, which were scattered behind her on the floor, she touched the rim of a glass vase and gently pulled it towards her.

She held the vase in her hands, the very same vase. Rinsing off the years of dust, debris and a couple of dead spiders, she then filled it with water. She trimmed the roses as Tilly had shown her back in the workroom of the outbuilding and arranged them in the vase. When she stood back to admire them, she was enveloped in a big hug.

"Oh, what, Rose, you are getting good at this. Do you want to work for me?" Tilly and Harriet were at the doorway and Tilly was giggling.

"I am deadly serious, you?" Tilly laughed.

"Where did you find such a beautiful rose? That is exquisite, not quite seen that shade before," Harriet asked.

Rose blushed and shook her head from side to side, she was keeping this quiet for now, until she had shared it with Tom. Roses were his passion and he deserved to know first. She hoped he would not be away for much longer; a garden evolved with the seasons and this year she was more involved in the garden than ever. The garden was becoming as special to her as the house. Her newly discovered rose was not something she wanted to discuss on the phone. She didn't want to send him a photo either. Maybe he had already spotted this plant, she was sure it hadn't bloomed before. She wouldn't have missed something as special as this, would she?

She was dying to show Tom. She needed him with her again. Maybe she would go against all her principles and ask him to come home. Ask him to live with her, settle in her house with her.

Harriet and Tilly waited patiently for Rose to tell them what they both wanted to know. Rose remained silent, keeping it to herself for now.

Chapter Thirty-Eight

"Why are you both here and on a Sunday too? Is everything OK, girls?"

"We are here to feed our little Mowzer as Mickey is over at Bob and Doreen's for Sunday dinner. Don't pull that face, Rose. Doreen is trying hard to make a friendship with Mickey and she thought Mickey was missing you."

Harriet giggled, as she interrupted again. "No, she thought Mickey was missing 'her' as apparently, they were always chatting when Mickey went into 'The Ship' for his daily pint. The old regulars are missing her, she says. I think it is her missing everyone's company and being a pub landlady. She used to gossip all day and now all she has to talk to is Bob."

"That's why Bob doesn't mind her going off gallivanting and working with Arthur these days, gets her out from under his feet and gives him some peace and quiet. He doesn't seem to miss the landlord days at all and loves the slower, quieter pace of their new life."

Rose grinned at Tilly and Harriet who were now firm friends from sharing their workspace. Without her business plans they would never have met or worked together. But where was Mowzer? He was normally such a gannet for food and Rose was sure he would have rushed out to find her if he was close. She was curious as to why Tilly and Harriet were crossing the drive to her utility room. "Oi, you two, where were you going?"

"Mowzer is being fed in the utility room so we could keep the house all locked up. Mickey was worried about locking Mowzer in by accident, or more to the point Mowzer having an accident in the house!"

"Surely that wouldn't be a problem with everyone around in the daytime, leaving a window ajar for the little devil. Where is he?"

"We were here this morning, dropping some stuff off after a wedding fayre yesterday, before we went to that trendy pub on the seafront for lunch and a couple of cheeky wines. He was about then, dozing in the sun." The trio arrived at the utility room. "Ah, look, there he is."

Mowzer stretched out on the countertop where he had been having his afternoon snooze. His front legs stretched out in front of him with his bum high in the air. He waggled his tail at the women and then jumped down to their feet ready for his meal. Rose plucked him off his feet and cuddled him tight. She buried her face in his fur. Mowzer tried to clamber onto her shoulder as if he were still a kitten and could fit there. She extracted his paw from the material of her T-shirt and scolded him gently, whispering into his ear. He rubbed his head and neck against her mouth and purred with delight. His attention wavered and he jumped out of Rose's arms when Tilly opened the fridge. The fridge reeked of fish. Wrinkling her nose, she said, "My Joe's special concoction for his little black and white friend. We didn't want him going missing while you were away, so we came up with this plan between us. Our Mowzer hasn't been going very far from this fridge since his special dishes have been on his menu."

Rose laughed. "They know how to make a fuss of you, don't they? You know where your home is, don't you? So do I, it's right here. You two don't need to drive home, do you? Come with me and share the home-cooked food that my mum has sent me home with. There is a bottle of wine right here."

"That would be lovely, a real girlie night in. Shall we call the others and see if they want to join us? Not Doreen as she is busy plying Mickey with Sunday dinner and beer. What about Ashley and Sue? I think Pearl has a function on tomorrow. She said something about an event in the library where she was making 50 cupcakes to order with a book motif in the middle of each of the cakes. We suggested a chocolate frosting and she brought some of the chocolate cupcakes in for us all to try on Friday. Oh, Rose, you should have been there. None left for you, I am afraid, they all went. We didn't know when you were coming back," Harriet said.

Tilly giggled, as the wine in her stomach was not being soaked up by the meal they had earlier. She kept giggling. "That was Harriet's excuse for eating the last couple."

"You weren't supposed to tell her that, you," Harriet snapped back.

Rose rummaged in the fridge for the wine and howled when she realised that she had left all her mum's cooked treats in the car in the sun. Giggling at Tilly and Harriet's antics, she ran out to retrieve them.

She rushed headfirst into someone walking up the drive. He grabbed her firmly by the shoulders and put his head down to kiss her on the cheek. Rose was startled at first, but when she saw who it was that had kissed her tenderly, she lifted her mouth to his for a proper kiss.

Knowing the girly night was not going to happen now, Tilly and Harriet crept past unnoticed behind the couple, clambered into Tilly's car and drove off without even saying goodbye. They would have their girlie night another time when they could get all the saucy details of this moment and what was to come. As they expected, the couple didn't notice their departure at all.

For Rose was lost in the moment.

Chapter Thirty-Nine

How odd, that both Tom and Rose decided to return to the house on the same afternoon, unbeknown to each other. Both of them were deep thinkers and neither of them had really been away from the house at all. Tom had similar dreams to Rose, nothing as revealing as a snapshot of the house in the past in all its glory. He, in contrast to Rose, had dreams that centred on the garden, the specimen plants that the Captains had found and brought back from their travels or haggled from other plant collectors in ports and cities across the world. Plants that they had brought back as a symbol of their love and affection for the women in their lives. The house was a constant backdrop in the riot of colour from the rich tapestry of shrubs, trees and roses that were the ladies' pride and joy, ever present in his dreams.

Their dreams had prompted Tom and Rose to return to the house and be back together. Tom was shocked that he had been away so long. As he drove up the lane, he could see the hedgerow vegetation was twice as high due to the outstanding summer weather. It was not often the British weather in summertime was perfect, but this year there was an equal measure of rain and sunshine and everything that could grow was growing fast. He had seen Rose park her car and wander straight into the garden. He parked his van in the lane, to give Rose some space and to see who was there with her. He wanted her on her own and didn't want to share her with anyone.

Tilly and Harriet didn't see his van parked in the lane when they arrived as they approached from the other direction. He didn't think they would stay long, but when he overheard their plans for a girlie night, he knew he needed to act fast.

He had made sure that Rose walked straight into him when he saw she wasn't really looking where she was going and couldn't resist the kiss. He had no real strategy to change her plans, but his impulsive move had the desired effect. He saw Tilly and Harriet diplomatically leave them to it over Rose's shoulder out of the corner of his eye.

He had Rose all to himself, just the way he liked it. With a grin, Tom tried to manoeuvre her into the house, but ever practical Rose made a beeline to her car first to pick up all the food that her mum had carefully made and packed for her. She loaded Tom up with carrier bags and then manoeuvred him over to the fridge and freezer in the utility room instead. Tom accepted the change of direction with a wry smile.

Mowzer having been fed by Tilly had vanished, leaving the smell of his fishy dinner behind. Wrinkling his nose, Tom looked at Mowzer's clean plate on the floor and carefully stepped around it to pack the food away for Rose. Rose bustled about behind him, growing impatient with his clumsy attempt to pack the food in the limited space available. She grabbed the bottle of wine and took it back to the house with her. It was only then she realised that Harriet and Tilly had tactfully sneaked away.

Returning to the kitchen, Rose poured the wine into two glasses and passed one to Tom.

He didn't take it from her. He plucked the vase with her newly picked roses from the sink, brandishing it at her as if it were a wine glass with a regal wave and smelling the scent as if it was a rare vintage.

"Rose, where did you get these from? I have never seen a rose of this colour before, with this beautiful scent. I have a rare rose in my van that I sourced from an old garden near to my parents' house. It is not in flower and in a bit of a sorry state. It was my present to you, after being away for so long. I really didn't mean to be, but one thing led to another, like it does. My new rose is not going to cut it, you have these beauties. OMG, please tell me they were not a gift from someone else. I asked Steve to look after you while I was away as I didn't know how long I was going to be. He made a move on you, didn't he? Really, with roses too. I am going kill him, I thought he was my mate."

Rose raised her eyebrows and felt herself getting cross with Tom. He had only just come back and stirred the very bones of her with just the one kiss but had the cheek to think that she would look elsewhere when he had not been gone that long. She opened her mouth to yell at him, but closed it quickly, when her brain caught up. She blushed when she remembered Steve and what he had meant to her lately. Had Tom caught the vibe, seen her blush? She hoped not.

Chapter Forty

She couldn't keep a lid on all her emotion, and some had to escape.

"Tom, you are blaming Steve again even when you asked him to look after me. Look after me. I am not some pet that needs looking after. I am a strong, independent woman."

"Strong, independent woman, really? You didn't stay here alone for long, did you? First you had Lisa to stay even when you should have gone away with me and then you went running home to mummy and daddy a few days ago. You didn't want to leave the house when you had the chance with me and then you leave it on a whim when I am gone."

Rose took the vase from Tom's hands, because she didn't want him to hold it. He looked as if he was going to throw it at her. He was mad, angry even. Rose put the vase down carefully on the countertop next to the kettle, took a big slurp of wine from her glass and headed into the garden.

Tom was left in the kitchen. He wanted to storm out and carry on arguing with Rose and debated going back to his apartment above his brother's restaurant to calm down. Instead, he walked down the drive to get his van and then parked up and started unloading more plants from the back to join the many that were already lined up outside the outbuildings. He then busied himself watering them all and checking them over.

They had gone from being lost in the moment to being together but detached in every which way. The house and gardens were quiet. Tom was busy with his plants, cross with himself for losing his rag and with his plans of romancing Rose after time away in tatters. Rose was sat with her back on the trunk of the apple tree looking back at the house, while sipping her wine. She could hear Tom with his plants and wished that he was there with her. She wasn't going to make the first move; she was leaving that to him.

When Tom realised that Rose was not going to come and find him, he knew he had to eat humble pie and seek her out. He went back to the house; he was hungry and fancied some of the cold meat, pastries and pies he had put in the fridge for Rose. He thought she would have come inside to get some more wine or maybe a cuppa, but the wine was untouched, and the kettle was cold when he checked the kitchen.

Surely, she wouldn't still be in the garden, he thought, as he looked out of the front window to see if he could see her. He looked across at the bench where she loved to sit with Mowzer but that was empty. He cast his eyes back around the room when he didn't see her. The room had changed so much since he had been away. Rose had been back in the house as she had placed the vase in the middle of the dining table. The carpet he was standing on, was exquisite and looked very expensive. The over-mantel mirror looked perfect above the fireplace. He was amazed that they had managed to find more of the green wallpaper Rose had loved so much, and managed to make good the walls and paper the entire room.

The old oak door was open wide. It was a heavy door, but it was swaying as if someone had just left the room. He crossed the room to open the door wider to see what or who was there, but all he found was the bricked-up cavity. He noticed the clock that was standing to the left of the fireplace next to the window. He touched the polished patina of the wood and raised his hand to the clockface. He felt the vibrations of the steady tick and the pendulum swaying back and forth in the body of the clock. As he touched it the tick got louder and the pendulum swung faster and faster. The oak door on the other side of the fireplace slammed shut with all the other doors in the house. The house trembled and shook.

Tom was covered in dust as the vibrations gathered apace. He recoiled as the clock chimed the hour. His whole body shook, he trembled and fell to the floor, one hand holding his head, the other twitching at his side. Something was clearly very wrong.

Chapter Forty-One

A glass of wine and a couple of hours of sunshine after a long drive home had worn Rose out. The cool breeze through the boughs of the old tree brought welcome relief from the heat. She had dozed off, while mulling over what she and Tom had together and how much she loved him. She wished that they could sort it all out and she dreamt of the life she wanted with Tom. She was bustling in the kitchen and laughing over in the studios in the outbuildings with her friends trying to learn a new craft or technique. Mowzer was present in every scenario that she dreamt of, and it all felt very real, until she heard the clock chime.

The chime was loud and the vibrations from it made the apple tree tremble and shook her awake. She was facing the front of the house and saw Tom in the front room, touching the clock in the corner. She saw him recoil from the clock as if it was hot to touch and had burnt him. She saw the two ladies of the house burst through the oak door to be at his side, tenderly nursing him as he lay there.

She got up and watched from the window as the ladies tenderly stroked him and remained at his side until he started to stir. They came to the window to her, with tears in their eyes they whispered, "Love him, my dear, before it is too late. Love him, we beseech you," before they faded away.

Rose sobbed as she rushed into the house, through the front door that was inexplicably unlocked and open wide for her. She fell to her knees and cradled Tom's head in her hands as he regained consciousness. She had done the same for Mickey when he fell up at the folly in the snow and here, she was doing the same thing with someone else she loved in the house. The only difference was she saw what happened this time. She still had no clue what happened to Mickey at the folly.

Tom came to and tried to stand almost immediately. Rose clutched him tight and told him to stay still.

"Rose, I feel fine. I don't know what happened, but I feel fine. How did I end up on the floor? But it's nice that you are here. Rose, where has the carpet gone? Why is the mirror on the floor? Where is my clock, my clock? Oh, it is in my van. I thought it was there, over there. Rose, Rose? Are you listening to me?"

Rose couldn't make sense of his ramblings as the room was as empty as it was when she had left to visit her mum, apart from the door. It had been uncovered while she was gone. Looking around her, she noticed a scrap of the wallpaper on the table. She surmised that it must have been Steve who had uncovered the door, for that was the type of thing he would do for her. He knew she liked the wallpaper and wanted to get it reproduced for the room. He was so lovely. Tom was still muttering about his clock. He pulled himself from Rose and stood up, brushing himself down. He was covered in dust but on closer inspection it was ash, not dust. Wood ash by the smell of it.

Rose helped him brush the ash off his clothes and sniffed hard.

"Wood ash. Is this ash, do you think? Why are you covered in ash? I haven't been burning wood in here, but I have been plagued by smoke, you know."

Tom was still going on about his clock and his van.

"Rose, the clock is in the van but it belongs here, come with me and see. I found it for you with other things at a boot fair near my mum and dad's house. They said it was from the big house that is being demolished, where I got the plants from. All your new plants. Please come and see them, Rose. I am fine, I don't know how I ended up there. Forget it and stop looking at me as if I am some precious porcelain. Rose, please!"

With a last look to check if the ladies were still there and listening hard for any whispers, she left the room. When she got to the doorway, she heard the whispers again. "Love him, my dear, before it is too late. Love him, we beseech you."

Chapter Forty-Two

Rose tried to steer Tom towards the sofa or the armchair in the back room, thinking that the soothing sound of water running past the house would calm him down. She needed him to sit down so she could reassure herself that everything was well. She thought he had died in front of her and was joining the ghostly ladies for eternity. She was heartbroken at the thought of him leaving her. Their differences were a yawning chasm earlier in the day when they were both far away from the house and each other, but now they were together in the house, they were less obvious.

Tom clearly thought the world of her, thought Rose, as she stared at the man at her side. She had lost sight of that. She thought he loved the garden more than her, but maybe, just maybe they were equal in his eyes. She would take that, definitely take that. She loved him after all. The words of the ladies rang in her ears, as the words of the Captains had done in the past. The Captains had never steered her in the wrong direction and had often showed her the way.

"Love him, my dear, before it is too late. Love him, we beseech you." The whispers followed her, the voices insistent and demanding. The 'too late' part made no sense. What were they implying by 'too late'? Was Tom ill? Was something about to happen? What could she do?

Tom didn't want to sit down and pushed Rose aside when she tried to gently push him through the doorway of the room. He wanted to show Rose the stuff he had been collecting little by little while he was away. He wanted to explain what had kept him from her and why, but only when she had seen for herself what he was talking about.

Rose and Tom ended up wedged in the hallway. Rose unwilling to let Tom leave the house and Tom doing his best to prise Rose off him. She was like a limpet on a rock and refused to relinquish her grip and shift her weight. They were both as stubborn as each other.

Tom dipped his head to kiss her, but she turned away from him. He was not trying that old chestnut in order to bend her to his will. She needed him to sit down, she needed to take a breath and the constant whispers to get out of her head and stop completely. The words were on a continuous loop, the same phrase over and over.

With a shove that belied her size, she managed to get Tom to topple into the armchair just inside the door and she perched on the arm. She held his shoulders with both hands to prevent him from putting his weight on his feet and getting the advantage again. He sat still and looked at her; his breath was heavy and rasping.

Watching him closely, her breath on his cheek, she watched as he calmed down. His breath grew steady and soft again.

As his breathing softened, so did the whispers. The sentence grew fractured in her head until the words, 'too late' were left.

"Too late... too late... too late." Over and over again...

When the whispering stopped, she took her arms away from his shoulders and with no constant pressure, Tom was free to pull Rose down onto his lap. He pulled her close and kissed her full on the mouth. His intention was obvious, his objective clear. Rose wasn't concerned for his health with the ladies' whispering silenced at last. She kissed him back with every ounce of her being.

Tom's mind was on other things now, thoughts of plants and

clocks forgotten. Rose didn't care where he had been for so long or wonder what he had been up to. He was there with her and in the moment that was all that mattered, that they were together.

They had the same intention as they climbed the stairs to bed. The back door shut quietly behind them in the kitchen and quiet footsteps followed them. The bedroom door was shut in a similar fashion with a heartfelt sigh and the tiniest whisper pronounced, "Love him, love him… That's right, my dear."

Chapter Forty-Three

Rose and Tom stayed in bed for the rest of the evening; they had no reason to get up and every reason to stay in bed. So, they did, they stayed wrapped in each other's arms in the time-honoured tradition of lovers, letting the world pass them by. Enjoying each other again. The bedroom door was shut tight so even the meows of Mowzer wanting his supper were ignored.

The front side window was open and the breeze coming into the bedroom turned from hot, to warm and then to chilly before they realised that the light of the day had darkened, and dusk had long gone. Covering their naked bodies with the duvet Tom pulled Rose in close for one last lingering kiss, before announcing that he was going downstairs to find something to eat.

"Oh, Tom, brilliant idea, I am starving. You better put some clothes on first!"

"Rose, don't be daft, there is no one here but us. I am not going to bother, you know. Take a look at this butt!" He wiggled his bum at Rose on his way past the end of the bed, and opened the door to an angry, very hungry male cat, who launched himself at Tom at speed. With one hand clutched over his manhood and the other fending off Mowzer, he stumbled backwards onto the end of the bed with Mowzer perched on his bare chest. Before Tom could scoop Mowzer from his chest and unceremoniously deposit him back onto the floor with his free hand, Rose gathered him up and cradled him on her shoulder, cooing to him like a baby. When his back claws scrabbled for purchase on her bare breasts, she put him onto the floor with a yell.

"Methinks we should both get dressed before Mowzer does the pair of us any more harm. Let's go and see what we can nibble." Rose threw Tom's pants at him and wiggled into her own and pulled her T-shirt over her head. Tom took his pants from Rose, with a smirk. "Oh, Rose, something to nibble…"

A blushing Rose slung Tom's T-shirt at him next then pushed him away, feinting his next amorous advance. Then they both followed the silhouette of Mowzer as he galloped down the stairs in anticipation of his dinner.

Halfway down the stairs, he stopped abruptly and leapt onto the windowsill. He stretched his little body as far as it would go in order to peer out through the window, looking through the section of the stained glass depicting the rays of light from the lighthouse. Tom and Rose almost toppled down the stairs, but managed to stay upright and they looked out, to see what had managed to stop the cat on his way to food. The yard was in darkness, but for a few security lights that Steve had rigged up on the end of each of the buildings. They were motion-sensor, triggered by movement.

Mowzer chirruped in excitement and pawed at the glass. Tom and Rose saw nothing but continued to look hard at the yard. They were missing something that Mowzer could clearly see. Until shadows appeared in the light. A man and a woman were walking together up the driveway, into the courtyard towards the path to the folly. The man had his arm around the lady. The figures were not walking in the light, so just the silhouettes of the couple were visible. A cloud of pipe smoke billowed over them.

Mowzer dropped onto all four feet and continued his descent to the kitchen. Rose and Tom followed him, sharing his haste. Keen to see more than just shadows. Opening the back door for Mowzer, quietly and quickly, Rose saw Mowzer rush out of the house in order to catch them up, trampling over her bare toes in his haste to get out. Pulling Tom behind her, she ran out into the courtyard, not giving a thought to their lack of clothes and the coolness of the night air.

The couple rounded the old oak tree at the very start of the footpath to the folly and faded out of sight as Tom and Rose left the house. Rose broke into a run, desperate to catch them so she could see if it really was her Captain and his lady and that they were together again. Not apart.

When her bare feet touched the damp soil of the footpath, she stopped with a shudder. It was so dark in front of her she couldn't see where and what she was stepping on. She grabbed the trunk of the old oak and looked hard into the blackness.

There was a flash as if someone had switched on the light, for all of a second. A flicker, if that. She saw the couple walking, accompanied by Mowzer scampering at their feet, for all intents and purposes like a small dog. Nosing here and there and running back to the man's side. Practically glued to the man's trouser leg every couple of strides, the cat getting as close as he could. The man never looked down but glanced to his side frequently. Mowzer was never kicked, the three of them were in perfect unison. The acrid pipe smoke wafted back on the cool breeze.

Tom missed the flicker of light and didn't see what Rose and Mowzer had seen on the stairs. He had followed Rose, to keep her safe and to see what all the fuss was about. Wrinkling his nose, he said, "Rose, what's that smell? It often follows me round the garden when I am working out there. Very putrid but comforting… really comforting. After all that fuss where the hell is Mowzer? Did he come this way? Why have you stopped?"

Rose pointed ahead into the darkness and for a very brief second the footpath was illuminated once more. The smoke visible in the damp night air with Mowzer trotting along on his own. His furry face looking up at his master from time to time, although the Captain could no longer be seen.

Chapter Forty-Four

Tom blinked once and grabbed Rose.

"I love Mowzer dearly, but what an idiot marching off like that instead of eating his dinner. I have worked up an appetite, Rose, this way. I am not walking to the folly in just my underpants and T-shirt, not even for you. Rose, Rose."

Rose ignored him and stood staring into the blackness and then into the hedgerow. She crossed the footpath and reached out to touch the leaves of the old tree opposite. She pulled a lump of foliage from the branch and pushed it into Tom's hand.

"This is the most amazing tree, and it looks so spooky and weird in the darkness right now, doesn't it, Tom? You can hardly see it. You know it is there, you can hear and almost feel it is moving like a real person. It rustles. It would be a good place to hide, don't you think?"

"Rose! No one is hiding in the tree, although if you approach it from the other side, it has a hollow trunk like the ones in the garden. There seems to be a boundary of these trees all around the property, surely you have noticed them before. I know they were not on my 'look after' list but really, Rose, what are you like?" he teased. "They are very old, you know, Rose. Very, very old. There was probably a well-maintained yew hedge sometime in the garden's history as the trees don't seem to be planted randomly. That yew was probably here before the house. Some people believed that yews marked a pagan site, as a yew tree has the unusual ability to virtually live forever. Let's talk about your yew trees inside. I know it is the summer, but I am getting really chilly. Come over here, you."

Pulling Rose close, he marched her towards the house, stopping along the way to pick up some bits from the utility room fridge and freezer. Noticing that all Mowzer's feeding stuff was out there, Tom topped up his bowl with dry kibbles.

When he got back to the house, Rose was not in the kitchen waiting for him; he surmised that she had gone back to bed. When he arrived in the bedroom with a tray, containing lots of different stuff to nibble as a suppertime meal, he was surprised to see that she wasn't in bed. The curtains weren't drawn so he could see the garden outside without moving from the bed. He looked out once more into the blackness. He hadn't switched on the bedroom light, just leaving the landing light on to cast a glow onto the bed. This meant that he could see out and not his reflection in the glass as he would if he had the main light on.

There in the darkness, was Rose wandering in the garden, looking for the yew trees she had asked him about earlier. He caught sight of her in the distance and saw that she had found the largest tree on the property, which was at the very far corner of the garden, not far from where the old beech tree had fallen. But when she stepped into the void in the middle of its hollow trunk she disappeared from his sight. Tom knew that the void was there and had stood and pondered the wonder of the ancient tree himself weeks earlier. He couldn't help but be worried about Rose, out there alone where he could not watch over her anymore.

He munched a biscuit and kept watch, waiting for her to come out. She spent enough time in the heart of the cavernous tree to make him worried. He stopped absentmindedly munching her mum's home baked biscuits, scattering crumbs into the bed, and willed her to come out and back to bed.

Rose didn't stay in the hollow for too long as she couldn't see a thing. She felt the contours of the tree with her fingers and wished she had a torch. She didn't know why she was wandering around the garden in the middle of the night on her own but had an inkling that the yew trees were the key to 'everything'. Glancing back at the house and then up at the window she saw a shape in the half light of the bedroom. Her Tom was back in bed but watching over her.

Knowing that Tom was watching her nocturnal wanderings, she felt silly to be traipsing around the garden in the dark. She crept along the edge of the garden and up the path that she mistakenly thought, and Tom believed, led to nowhere. Remembering the events of the day she quickened her pace and walked with renewed purpose.

Her intention provoked the main house to reveal itself in its glory once more; the snapshot in time replayed again. She was not alone in the garden anymore. The house was busy too. She recoiled when she brushed past a gardener bent over a rose with pruning shears in his hands. The gardener raised his cap in greeting when he stood up and his eyes met hers.

She smiled at the gardener. "I thought you were in bed, Tom, now is not the time for pruning roses! You don't have to doff your cap at me, my love." She giggled and went on. "I suppose I am the 'lady' of the house."

Tom listened to her chatter from the window above. He was perplexed by the conversation.

Who was she talking to and giggling with and why did she call him Tom!

Rose clambered into bed next to Tom absolutely exhausted from her night-time gardening. She grabbed a savoury biscuit and piled it high with cheese. "That will make you dream, Rose," Tom warned, "or have you already done your dreaming in the garden? Who were you talking to, Rose? I wasn't out there. Why were you talking to me?"

"I know you weren't, silly, I saw you moving about in the window and guessed you had gone back to bed. I don't know what I was thinking about looking for old trees in the dark. I need to show you this."

Reaching into her pocket she pulled out a tattered, loosely bound book and an old pencil, chewed at the end. The dents from the teeth of its owner marked a ring of splintered wood at the end. Her eyes rolled as she passed it to Tom, and she leant back into the pillows and into the headboard of the bed.

"He dropped this for me, for you. It's Tom's. It's yours, my love, yours."

Chapter Forty-Five

Tom spent the rest of the night reading the book that Rose had handed him. Rose was totally disinterested and after munching enough to sate her hunger, she pushed the tray aside and curled up beside him to sleep. He could feel her body heat next to his as he leant into her and tried to decipher everything in the book.

The writing was illegible but very similar to his own, so he could make out odd words. It was the gardener's book, planting dates and times, lists of new specimens and the rough plans of the original garden with later pages, showing the changes and how the garden was evolving. It stopped abruptly, three quarters of the way towards the back of the book. The remaining pages blackened with age and soot. Within the pages, the yews were marked, the boundary, the beds, the house.

This was the first time Tom had seen the house, the larger house that had disappeared from living memory, its very existence missing completely.

It was all becoming clear to him; the very evidence was there in his hands at last. The larger house, the path to the main entrance, the blocked-up doorway. How could he have missed it?

As dawn broke, Tom hadn't slept at all. He had crept downstairs and out to his car to retrieve his bag and his laptop, the modern equivalent of the notebook. He balanced the laptop on his knees when he got back into bed and the notebook on the side of Rose's body as she lay next to him. He compared his newly acquired plant list with those in the old book. They were identical, he could restore the garden as it was with all his new plants. Technically the plants weren't new, they were the remnants of other more established plants dug up from the soon-to-be-built-on garden near his parents'. He hoped they would all survive the transition from garden to garden, but they would if he started soon. He had anticipated a couple of days of searching for the old paths and clues in the old garden. He and Rose had the same idea, but he had no clue why and how Rose had hit on the yew trees at the same time with the odd notion of exploring the garden in the darkness. He had been planning to stand at each of the old yews to get his bearings before trying to figure out the intricacies of the old garden, but it had all fallen into his lap literally, after Rose's nocturnal wanderings and little old Mowzer showing them the way.

Tom grinned. Mowzer had been off to the folly and the yew tree that Rose had wrenched a lump from, was only just on her land. It was odd, that Mowzer hadn't taken her to the hollow yew tree in the garden, as that tree was Tom's favourite and he often saw Mowzer there. He was hoping to get Rose to put a little seat or bench in there. It was where he went when he wanted to have a think about things and wanted to be alone. He was slightly miffed that Rose had found it. Looking down at the sleeping Rose, she still looked shattered after her nocturnal walk. Would she remember the tree? Or how she got the old book? She must have had it in the house and thought of it when she got in. Her sleepy ramblings had said something different. What did she say again, something about it being Tom's, and that he had dropped it?

Tom hadn't seen it before and the book was so precious to him now, he would never drop it. He folded his laptop and put it on the floor beside the bed. He gently picked up the little book from the duvet that was stretched across Rose as she was laying on her side. With the book still in his hand, he snuggled down next to Rose and pulled her close. Without a sound Mowzer jumped up and lay in front of her. Drowsily she reached out and stroked his head. Purring happily, Mowzer curled up in a ball with his head resting on his hind legs and fell into a deep sleep. Tom leaned across Rose and whispered to Mowzer, "I know where you have been, my man," as he picked several yew leaves from his fur. "Not you as well!"

Chapter Forty-Six

Rose and Tom slept late the following morning. Mowzer joined them in their slumbers, ignoring the signs from his hungry stomach. The tom cat was always hungry, and his size had started to match his large appetite. But for now, he was fast asleep after his night-time adventures and because he was asleep, his human companions had enjoyed a much needed lie in.

Rose awoke in Tom's embrace, his arm cradling her to him, his steady breath in her ear. She lay there for a while enjoying his company and thankful that he had returned to her. She couldn't lie still for long, so she gently pushed him over onto the other side of the bed and sat with her knees under her chin. She watched him sleep and couldn't help but notice that his hands were dirty with streaks of mud all over them. His fingernails were filthy with earth under every nail and the very tips of his fingers black right down to the knuckle. It looked as if he had been digging with his bare hands in the garden. She wouldn't put it past him, but hoped he hadn't.

When she couldn't get comfortable, she shifted each buttock until she realised that she was sitting on a book. Pulling it from underneath her, she held it in her hands and stared. Where had this come from? Flicking through the pages, it became clear that the book was a gardener's journal. On closer inspection, it was a journal, but it belonged to her garden. It was fascinating. She turned the pages from the back to the front as she usually did when reading a magazine or reference book for the first time. She always went from the back of the book to the front. Constantly teased for this reading habit, she glanced across at Tom to check he was still asleep. He was, but Mowzer was watching her with one eye wide open. Knowing that he wouldn't judge her, she continued to flick through the pages.

She was shocked to discover that the book was not complete as she had first thought, and that it looked as if it had sustained fire damage. The sooty and burnt pages were fragile and as she handled them bits of parchment sprinkled over the bed sheets. As she turned the pages, she saw the main house depicted, the yews, the path and the outbuildings. All the big trees were marked, including the beech tree that had only recently fallen.

She was so engrossed that she failed to notice Tom was awake.

"I see you have found the notebook again. Where did you find that last night? It was almost pitch black when you were wandering around the garden on some mad hunt for yew trees. You said that Tom gave it to you, but I was here in bed watching you. Where did you find it? Tell me, Rose."

"I haven't seen this wonderful little book before, Tom. Look, it is our garden with the house as it once looked." She waved the book under his nose and grinned broadly.

He grinned back at her. "You gave that book to me, Rose, don't you remember? Last night after we followed Mowzer all the way to the yew on the way to the folly in our underpants and T-shirts."

"Just kidding, Tom, I know we went off to the folly, but then I came back to bed, didn't I? I remember talking to you though. It was you, I know it was, I would recognise you anywhere and you were wearing a cute little flat cap and you doffed it at me like I was the lady of the house. It was so funny." She giggled as she remembered it.

Tom knew they were at cross purposes, but he didn't want to

contradict Rose's recollection of the evening. He was still desperate to show her his new plants. It didn't matter how or who found the notebook, he reasoned, as long as he had it.

He needed it back so the next time she waved it under his nose, he grabbed it and her, knocking Mowzer to the floor as they tussled.

Several hours later, after a very late breakfast, Tom showed his new plants off to Rose. He was like a father showing off his new baby or a child that was showing off what they had made at school. He marched Rose up and down the line of plants. He caressed their leaves, stroking their stems as if they were cherished friends or lovers. He referred to his newly acquired notebook as he came to each plant, smiling that each and every one was included in the garden plan.

Rose patiently listened to Tom exalt the delights of his new plants and was thrilled when he explained that he was gifting them all to her for her garden. He was so excited, so vocal that it was all Rose could do to stop him grabbing a spade and marching off to plant them there and then.

When Tom ground to a halt with a shriek, she barrelled into the back of him. "Oh my god, Rose. I think we have them all. All of them. Every single one. I did have the bigger ones sent on to the nursery site, but all of these fit. The garden I got them from was almost identical in everything but size, it was like this garden was a replica of it on a smaller scale."

He strode off towards his van and opened a door. Rose stared aghast at the contents. There was all manner of stuff that Tom had picked up from the boot sale and right there was the clock she had seen in the house. The very same clock that Tom had touched in the front room of the house. As it started to chime the hour, she yelled.

"Don't touch the clock, Tom!"

Chapter Forty-Seven

Tom backed away from the clock and pulled some crockery from a box to the side of it to show Rose, instead. She noticed that the plates were identical to the pile sitting in the back of the pantry. Trying hard to ignore the chiming and the primal urge to check that Tom was OK after the events of the night before with the very same clock, she picked through the box of crockery. Although some of it was the same, there were slight differences to others that she had found in the pantry. The fancy one she had used for the bake off with Mickey. The initials were different, the family crest missing on some. The gold gilt edging and the weight of them matched though.

How very odd, she thought, then turned to Tom to ask him where he came by all this stuff. There was pallor to his face. His eyes were glassy and unseeing. He slumped to his knees and reached to his left temple with his hand. There he stayed until the clock fell silent.

He stood up gingerly, still holding his head. "I don't feel too good again, Rose, but hang on, give me a minute. Oh, think I have it, oh no…" he cried as he threw up onto her trainers.

Wrinkling her nose in disgust at the smell of the vomit, Rose sat Tom down in the back of the van, taking care not to touch the clock. She slipped her feet from her trainers which were only loosely tied and threw them into the garden out of the way. Barefoot now as she knelt at his feet and looked up at him.

"Are you alright? Did you stuff all mum's biscuits and cakes while

I was sleeping last night? I took the empty plates downstairs this morning but didn't want to say anything. You got a headache? Why do you keep holding your head?"

Tom shrugged and took his hand away from his head. "I feel fine now but could use a glass of water after that. I'm so embarrassed, Rose, I will buy you a new pair, let's sling that pair away in the rubbish. I'm so sorry."

Before Rose could stop him, he picked up the heavy clock and placed it carefully on the gravelled drive beside her.

"Give me a hand to get this back into the house, it's bloody heavy, and I will tell you how I found it. It needs to be back where it belongs, I reckon."

After locking the van, the pair of them carried the clock back into the house. They didn't need to call directions to each other, as they both knew where they were going.

When the clock was standing in the alcove next to the fireplace in the front room, Rose backed away from it. Tom crouched close, pushing and pulling it straight and into place. Then he joined Rose in the middle of the room.

The clock was silent, there was no tick, no sign of life.

"There wasn't a key with the clock, Rose. I can't see if I can mend it or get it working again without a key!"

Tom was talking to himself as Rose was in the kitchen, taking her set of keys off the hook. The key to the folly was on there with two others. She couldn't find what they unlocked. One of them looked like it was the right size, so she was going to try it.

She tried the key and with a wiggle or two in the lock mechanism, it turned. She didn't really like the clock, it gave off a sinister vibe. Knowing that Tom was not going to leave the clock alone until he had a good go at getting it working again, Rose left him to it.

As she walked away from the room, the negativity lifted. She turned to check that Tom was feeling himself again and saw that he had the clock facing the wall, with anything that could be open, wide open. His mouth set in a line, his eyes squinted as he concentrated on getting the old clock to work again.

She wasn't sure she wanted the clock to work again, or even have it in her house. How odd that she had the key to the clock that Tom had found. Where had he found the clock? Did it belong here to her Captain? If it did, why did he find it elsewhere, along with lots of other stuff from her house?

She had a spare set of keys to Tom's van, so she took herself off to unload the crockery and have a nosy on her own at everything else. She clambered in the back, leaving the door swinging.

The van had been filled to the brim when it had plants in there as well, so there was plenty of room for Rose to get down one side now that all the plants were stood in her yard. She sat cross legged at the far end when she discovered a pile of old books, some dusty, some pristine. She spotted one that looked like the gardener's journal, and it certainly looked very similar, but this was a ship's log, so it was slightly bigger. Embossed on the cover, was the name of the ship, 'The Fortune'. She couldn't really read it, as it was almost illegible inside. The ink had dried out long ago. The leather covering was mottled and slightly damp to touch. She held it to her nose and sniffed; it smelt of the sea. She edged out of the van and into the fresh air.

She was met by the familiar smell of pipe smoke, a gruff guffaw and then a chortle.

"So, this is your ship, Captain?" Rose murmured the question.

"You are finding my fortune now, my girl, my fortune…" a deep voice answered.

Chapter Forty-Eight

Rose and Tom stayed up late into the night talking. Tom explained to Rose that he had visited an old garden, about to be developed and built on the site of an old manor house he noticed when he was driving to his mum and dad's.

He had seen the similarities to the Captain's garden straight away. He was invited to clear the land for the developers after they had seen his interest. He set to it straight away when he had seen the quality of the plants they were just going to get rid of. He knew that he could lose some planting as it may not survive the uprooting and replanting, but he wanted to try. He had a weird impulsion to do so, which he couldn't quite put his finger on.

He went on to explain that everything else he had got from a boot sale. The seller had remarked that it all came from the old manor house, so he bought the lot. He used the money he had earned from working for Trevor and Judy.

He couldn't bring himself to invest Trevor and Judy's money in his business so had moved it to a separate account. This account was now empty as he had used the lot to pay for the clock, books and everything else. It seemed important that he buy it. He didn't have a reason, other than he had a vague suspicion that it all belonged at the Captain's house and with Rose.

He confessed to Rose that he had asked Steve to look after her, as he was going to be gone longer than he anticipated.

"Steve must have thought that I was going mad, rambling on like a mad man of having to stay away. I don't think I made much sense to him, although he never said so, but he must have thought that I was terminally ill, now I come to think of it. The conversation we had was so very intense, and Steve sounded so serious when he said goodbye."

"Well, that explains a lot. Why didn't you tell me before?" she cried as she nudged him hard on the shoulder.

"I knew you would have wanted to come and see the old garden, and I didn't want you to. It felt like you weren't allowed. It felt personal. I needed to do it on my own, bring it all back to you." He started to ramble.

"Well now you have, and we can work it out together. Where was that old house? I wonder how it connects to this house. Why would the gardens be similar, unless it was a particular garden designer or collector maybe? Or could it be the Captain's ancestral home?"

"You could have hit the nail on the head with that. The Captain's home, yes, that makes sense. If he collected plants on his travels, he would take one home, that might explain why we have some of the plants here but not there and vice versa. Maybe he took one home to his mother and one to his wife here."

"You could be right. After all, he did travel the world and this garden is and was famed for its roses."

"If that is so, then why would the gardens not be the same, if the plants came off the same ship? Why would the Captain make his home in such a small cottage?"

"This house was once much bigger, the doorway in the front room proves it. The path in the garden that once led to the original front door. Our Captain had a substantial house here, befitting of his position of a sea captain. It looks as though the cottage was here first and remains here. The bigger house could have been an extension of the cottage."

As they mulled the 'what ifs' into the night, the shadows of the past grew brighter around them, as if they were confirming everything Rose and Tom were surmising. The bigger house was standing tall again, the women bustling about in the main hallway, arranging fresh roses in the vase on the shiny round table. The old 'rent table' where the tenants used to line up to pay their dues to their master and landlord.

Upstairs above their heads in the back bedroom overlooking the folly and the sea in the distance stood another lady watching the horizon through the telescope. Yet another woman was atop the folly with a lantern peering into the darkness too.

When Rose and Tom made their way to bed, the house settled down around them, seemingly at peace. Rose saw the figurehead through the open door at the top of the landing as she passed; she looked wet. When she touched her wooden figure, she was soaking wet, absolutely soaked through. She ran her fingers down her dress and then held her carved hands and posy of roses in hers. As their fingers touched, she felt a vibration, a joy, and closing her eyes she felt the thrill of cresting every new wave in calm and stormy seas. She felt it all.

When she took her hands away, she was as wet as the figurehead, but bone dry when she left the room.

Chapter Forty-Nine

Tom stayed for a few days, spending most of his time in the garden, using the old journal to plant the garden as it used to be. Some of the specimens were looking worse for wear, so he took cuttings of those and planted the older ones at the rear of the garden to revive. If they didn't make it hopefully the cuttings would take.

He stumbled across the rubble Rose had found along the boundary line and thought it looked very familiar. He was up at the back of the garden near the water when he saw Mickey and Bert on the other side. After waving at them to join him, he posed the question to Mickey when he stood beside him in the garden.

"Well, Mickey, where have I seen these bricks before? They look so familiar, I know the answer is staring me in the face. Help me out, won't you?"

"Why hello to you too, Tom. Why did you stay away so long, my man? Everything OK?" Mickey joked.

"Lots to talk about, Mickey, but answer the question first. It's bugging me, please." Tom was impatient for an answer.

Mickey raised an eyebrow then raised the other and let the silence hang. He was always ready for a laugh, and he knew that Tom would kick himself when he told him.

"Tom, why didn't you ask Rose? I bet she would know. Is everything OK with you two? I saw you were back, but thought you may have needed some 'alone' time?"

"Mickey stop stalling for time and teasing me. Just tell me, please," Tom implored.

"If you insist. Now think hard. If it is here, it's likely that it belongs to the Captain's house, don't you think? What other building belongs to the Captain here, mate?"

Tom thought hard. "Oh bloody hell, my man," he teased, using Mickey's mannerisms back at him, as he had worked out the obvious. "The folly. The folly is built from the rubble of the main house, of course it is. The folly. Doh, wait till I tell Rose."

Mickey laughed. "I am sure Rose has worked it out herself before you, my man." He added the emphasis on the 'my man' phrase back at Tom.

"Let's go and see." With a grin they both strolled back to the house to ask Rose.

Rose heard the men in the garden and was so pleased to hear Mickey's voice again. She guessed that he had stayed away to give her and Tom some space and was grateful for that, but thrilled that he had come over to see her again. She had missed him and Bert.

But Bert was not with them, they found him on the way back through the garden. He was sat at the foot of the rose bush on the other side of the blocked door. He looked so forlorn, just sat there waiting. When the men came over to him, his tail didn't wag, he didn't get up. It was as if he was not waiting for them, but for the ladies of the house he had visited when he went through the door. His ladies.

Rose called Bert to her with the promise of a biscuit. As soon as he sensed there was a biscuit actually in her hands, his tail resumed its happy wag, and he leapt up and around her, eager for a taste.

"Oh, biscuits for the dog or biscuits for us?" said Mickey, greeting Rose with a kiss on the cheek. "You do know that I prefer cake, don't you?"

"The kettle is on, you two, so I will make you a cuppa when we get in. What are you two chatting about? You look up to no good."

Tom put on his serious face. "Rose, do you know the rubble that is just along there?" He waved his hands in the vague direction of it. "Well, it looks familiar to me. Do you know where I have seen it before?"

"No, not really, I clambered all over it just before I paddled home that time, Mickey. Do you remember?" She grinned at Mickey.

"Rose, you paddled home, really! What are you like? Seriously. Mickey, tell her. She hasn't made sense of it all yet either."

Mickey licked his lips in anticipation, keen to share his local knowledge with Rose. "Oh, my dear, I thought you would have worked it out. I told Tom here you wouldn't need to be told. Rose, the stone is the same as that in the folly. I reckon the folly was built with the stone from the big house. This was a manor house centuries ago, wasn't it?"

"You knew there was a house here before and you didn't tell me, Mickey. Why not?"

"I thought you knew there would have been a house here for centuries, the plot size is far too big for the present cottage-type dwelling. A tiny dwelling wouldn't have needed a coach house, stables, barn and gardener's huts. Why, if you didn't use a coach, you would have a pony and trap surely and a sturdy old barn-type structure. The outbuildings would have been mainly wood, not stone."

In the last few days, Rose learnt more about the house than she had ever done. Her affinity for the house had grown stronger. She hadn't made the connection with the folly before, as she was blissfully unaware that there was once a bigger house on the land. She had taken the outbuildings for granted and not questioned that they were not in keeping with the small house, just assuming that because the house was owned by Captains, they would have needed more storage space.

The old friends had tea and cake in the garden and spent the afternoon catching up and chatting. Tom had taken it upon himself to drive out for some fish and chips for dinner, as no one felt like cooking. When he returned, he brought with him another old friend he had bumped into at the beach.

He had invited him to join them all for dinner. Rose was thrilled when she saw him clamber out of Tom's van. He would know some of the answers about the house for sure.

Chapter Fifty

Rose gave Christian a warm hug when he got up close and she could see who he was. He hadn't been seen since the incident when the beech tree fell, and she wished she had taken a mobile number or something then, so she could have contacted him to make sure he was alright.

They decided to eat their dinner out in the garden as it was still warm. Christian pulled up a chair and sat down next to Mickey. When she and Tom went into the kitchen to put the takeaways on plates and get the knives and forks and condiments, she told him how pleased she was.

"I thought you would be happy to see him, that's why I brought him home with the dinner."

Rose gave Tom a big kiss and hugged him too. "This day is shaping up to be one to remember. I love it when you surprise me."

"Well, I did see Steve too, but he looked a little busy with a stunning redhead, so I didn't bother him. He was sitting on the sea wall, eating alfresco. He knows how to give a girl a good time!"

Tom didn't notice Rose's crestfallen face, but Mickey did as she came back to the table.

"You OK, my girl? Something upset you?"

Pasting a smile back on her face, "Oh, Mickey, I am good and so happy to have my friends around me," she said and sought to put those odd feelings about Steve to one side until she was on her own again.

They munched their fish-and-chip dinner as they chatted about the developments in the village. Rose regaled Christian with the antics of the new occupants of the outbuildings and which new businesses were working out of them now. Christian, who spent his time in the outbuildings through the winter months for shelter when he was homeless, shared his experiences living on the property as a solitary affair, with no human company, just that of the wildlife around him.

Christian spoke of the silence, the darkness, the cold but the feeling of being loved despite being solitary, of someone looking out for him while he sorted himself out. His glimpses of the captains in the window.

When they finished dinner, Christian continued to speak of his time in the outbuilding while Rose mulled over something different, something connected but not relevant to the conversation. The conversation should have caught her interest, but her mind focused in on the keys. She had three keys on the keyring. Three.

One was for the big old door of the folly and the tiny one fitted the old clock that Tom hadn't managed to fix. What was the other one for? It must be as obvious as the stones that once belonged to the house and now the folly. Getting the spark of an idea, Rose excused herself from the table. Taking the keys from the hook, she went into the front room. Ignoring the clock that was giving her the heebie-jeebies, she focused on the door.

The old oak door had a lock. She knew it was a long shot, but she couldn't stop herself. She put the key in and turned it. There was no jiggling needed; the key turned like a knife in butter. Softly and smoothly.

As it did so, the clock started ticking again. It was not a regular tick. The clock sounded like it had the hiccups, and it was struggling for breath in between each hiccup. The intervals were irregular. Some ticks were loud and others she could barely hear. The clock sounded unwell. She tapped the clock face and peered in. The ticks steadied and slowed to a regular beat as the clock got back in time with the mechanism. Then the hands whirled around the clockface at a frightening speed, blurring the numbers, but the tick remained steady.

Back at the table, Tom shivered and put his hand to his head. He could feel it aching, as if he had been hit by something hard. He heard a crack reverberate. He turned his head when he heard the crashing all around him. He jumped up, knocking the table over in his confusion. As the plates, knives and forks rained down on him, Bert raced for cover into the house while Mickey and Christian raced to his side.

Hearing the commotion, Rose flew back out into the garden to see what all the noise was about and found it in disarray. Tom looked very pale but shrugged off Mickey and Christian's concerns and stormed off in the direction of his van.

The table was upended, and the leftover food was scattered across the lawn, being eating by the ever-hungry Mowzer. Bert had followed Rose back into the garden and leaving the fish for Mowzer, was scoffing as many chips as he could find using his nose to seek out the ones in the longer grass.

It was total chaos.

With a wave, Mickey motioned Rose to chase after Tom to see if he was OK. She caught up with him at the door of the van. He was searching in the pocket for his keys.

"I really don't think you should be driving right now, Tom. You feeling strange again? Come and sit down with us. I will get you a glass of water."

"Rose, I am fine, but maybe you are right about the driving. I think I will get myself," he emphasised the word 'myself', "a glass of water and then I think I will go to bed. I need a lie down."

He turned on his heels and strode off once more, in front of her. With an embarrassed grin, he marched past his friends. "I feel a bit odd, going to have a lie down, must have been the sun. A touch of sun stroke, I am sure. Be back out after a little nap."

Mickey, Rose and Christian sorted the table out and retreated into the back room away from the debris of the dinner, passing the kitchen on the way to leave the dirty dishes in the sink. Nothing was broken, but the jovial mood was spoilt.

Chapter Fifty-One

Christian took his time as he made his way to the back room. He could never quite get used to the fact that the house was lived in now and felt so different. Eventually, he joined the others in the back room but unable to settle, asked Rose if he could have a look around.

He got as far as the front room and stood and stared at the old doorway. The key was in the lock and the door was swinging open into the room. He could see that the doorway behind it was bricked up. The bricks were shimmering, producing a haze. A tremor ran across the floorboards and stopped at his feet.

Christian looked around at the room with interest. Rose had furnished it well, for it looked the same as it did when he used to peek through the windows when he saw the lanterns lit. The carpet was intricately patterned and the walls a dazzling green. The fire was lit in the grate and the old clock leaning at a comforting angle towards the chimney breast, as if it had one glass too many. The lanterns were shining brightly, and the table was decorated with a beautiful vase of roses. Even the air itself was welcoming, the smell of wood burning in the grate with the scent of the roses. The mirror was on the chimney breast itself. When he looked into its reflective surface, the face of a Captain looked back at him.

The Captain's hat was set square on his head, which overshadowed his eyes, and his face was in shadow. His expression was familiar, so much so that Christian, said a, "Hello, Captain," out loud.

The Captain smiled, tilted his head in greeting and faded from view as Christian heard a set of footsteps coming towards him with a heavy tread. He looked down and saw the outline of a pair of boots. When he looked up, he saw the table was no longer empty with just a vase of roses in the middle. There a was a Captain's hat, upturned. Nestled inside was a pocket watch and alongside it was an old black telescope, weathered and tarred.

He picked up the telescope and held the weight of it in both hands. He stretched it out until it was three times the size as each section was pulled out. He held it to one eye and looked out over the garden towards the lane. He focused the telescope on the old yew tree Rose had hid in the night before, just in time to catch a shadow dash out. It moved too quick for Christian to see who it was as he was not familiar with the focus on the old telescope.

The figure was blurred, but Christian saw the long skirts of a woman and saw the shape knelt down at the base of what used to be the upright beech tree. The shape turned to look at Christian, willing him to understand. He took the telescope from his eye, to check he was turning the right dial on the mechanism, and when he had sorted himself out, the shadow was gone.

He jumped high into the air when Rose called, "What are you doing with the Captain's telescope? Where did you find that? I found that in the antique shop ages ago. I think it belonged to my Captain, don't you think?"

"It was right here on the table with his hat, Rose," he replied as he swung round to face her. His feet made the floorboard creak. "Whoa, where has the carpet gone, Rose? The wallpaper?" With his eyes wide he took in the bare room. "Oh, Rose, where has it all gone?"

He crossed the room to the clock. "The clock is standing tall now, though. That's good, all mended."

Rose and Christian linked arms and went to join Mickey, who was waiting for them in the other room. They didn't need to talk about what he had or hadn't seen, or why the Captain's belongings had appeared on the table. They each knew there was a reason for everything in this quirky little house. Christian would share the lady he had seen crouched at the foot of the tree and Rose would share the things that weren't easy to explain to anyone else. They were of the same mindset, the same wavelength.

Chapter Fifty-Two

The same couldn't be said for Tom when he left the house the following morning. He was uncertain and a little slow. Rose wanted to take him to see a doctor for a check-up, but Tom was insistent that it was just sun stroke and that he had been working too hard. Rose was cross that Tom had left to go and have a holiday from the pressures of work but spent his time on another job and working twice as hard. Of course, she didn't tell him any of this, just bustled around him trying to get him to relax and leave the garden and everything else for another day.

All her attempts were in vain, and she only succeeded in getting him to go back to his flat for some peace and quiet and to escape her constant nagging. With a quick shower and an equally quick breakfast, he kissed her goodbye and took off in his van before she could change his mind.

Rose watched him go from the bench in the garden. His van spluttered and popped its way down the road as if it had a mind of its own and was reluctant to move, but she heard Tom pumping the accelerator madly in his haste to get home.

She sat back to watch the antics of the magpies that were darting from tree to tree and bush to bush, playing 'chase' as it were. They held her attention and took her mind off Tom. They hopped across the grass, swooping and diving in a stunning display of aerobatics. The flashes of black and white with flashes of their fabulous bright blue feathers made her forget Tom for a while and allowed her mind to slow. The house seemed to comfort her again in its own unique way.

She didn't see Tom for a couple of days after that, but he spoke to her regularly every couple of hours or so. Rose suspected he was staying away because he wanted to clear some of the backlog that his absence from his business had created. He knew that Rose would hate it, if she thought he was unwell, so he was open and honest, but made it so that Rose couldn't do a thing about it. He insisted he felt one hundred percent fine and told her he had to catch up on lots of work and a ton of admin. He told her he had jobs, just not where they were and kept his whereabouts close to his chest so she couldn't just turn up and whisk him away. He worked long days until it was dusk for his regular customers. He was stubborn and should really have asked Steve or someone to help him with some of the bigger jobs, but he was tackling it all on his own.

Rose had her mind elsewhere; she knew that the house was speaking to her again, it its own imitable way, and knew that she just needed to follow the clues. After seeing the Captain's hat and telescope on the table, she started to make a pile of things she surmised had belonged to him. Then she started to make a separate pile of all the items that belonged to the women who had lived in the house.

She did the same thing in the kitchen, with the crockery. There was barely room to swing a cat anyway in her tiny galley kitchen. There was hardly any countertop left after she had piled on the crockery and old silver that had come from Tom, or she had found in the back of the large pantry.

In the outbuildings, she pulled the sailcloth from the pile of furniture in the large loft space where she and Lisa found the mirror. Now she knew the manor house had existed and the property had once been bigger, it all started to fit. The discarded furniture was all that remained from the bigger and older house. Some of it looked antiquated and sad, but other pieces looked almost in the prime of life, just needing some tender loving care again.

All the bigger items would have had to go in via the large doors in the rear of the loft space to store it. She was still puzzled as to when and why the manor house had been pulled down or left in disrepair.

In the only legible parts of the ship's log of 'The Fortune', were the figures, vast sums of money in those days. 'The Fortune' had certainly made her Captain a very wealthy man so where was the house that befitted his status?

Her wanderings took her all over the house and brought back fond memories of her first days there, with the Captain's hat falling off the mantelpiece announcing his presence. Her first Christmas in the house with Tom. The carvings that didn't quite make sense but seemed to point the way to using the outbuildings to make some money. The fallen beech tree and the battered box of precious items concealed within its roots that connected one of the Captains to his lady. There wasn't much remaining of her old aunt, but Rose guessed that her aunt had been all tied up with the history of the house, much like she was.

She rarely ventured to the clock. She heard its steady tick from every room of the house but noticed that it hadn't chimed an hour since it was stood up. The chiming was sinister, it frightened her on an inner level, and she really didn't like it.

So, when the clock chimed the hour, Rose froze. Every sense was on high alert and although she was in one of her favourite places, curled up in the window seat overlooking the river, she felt the chill. The coldness enveloped her.

The clock chimed and everything else was silenced. The water made no sound as it trickled and flowed across the stones below the window. The birds stopped singing.

Rose heard a noise, the sound of splintering wood and a loud crack. A shrill cry and gut-crunching thud as if something had hit the ground.

Chapter Fifty-Three

The ancient beech tree was identical in every way to the one that had toppled over in the Captain's garden, several months before, in the winter. The gnarled beech tree was all that remained of the neglected garden, as Tom had taken all of the plants to Rose's. The yellow diggers were parked in a row on the land outside, ready to move on Monday to start the foundations for the new estate that was being built. This garden was set to be lost forever.

Tom had sneaked back in for a last look at the land and to see if there was any tangible evidence left to connect this garden with the old Captains. The beech tree was one of several of the old trees that the developers had agreed to work around to maintain their 'green' credentials. Tom was sat not underneath the tree but beyond the edge of its crown. He didn't want to be shaded by the foliage, he wanted to sit in the sun.

He didn't know why he was there.

He wanted to get it all sorted in his head, but he was missing the last piece of the jigsaw. He just couldn't find it. He loved this garden with the same passion as the Captain's garden. He was sure they were connected. It was obvious, but he couldn't prove it. He needed to prove it. Not just to himself but to Rose. He needed to know.

When he listened hard, he caught a faint conversation and the sound of a wailing woman. The sound faded in and out, like the frequency needed tuning. He closed his eyes to focus on the sound with no distractions. He got the gist of the conversation without catching all the words. The woman was the mother, pleading for her son not to leave. He told her he was leaving to be with his only love, despite her status, and he would make his life elsewhere. He wanted to be happy, not just at the whim of his father who forbade the love. He was denying his birth right, his inheritance, but he would continue to sail the seas like his forefathers before him. The ship belonged to him now, so his father couldn't deny him his livelihood.

The mother's sobbing quietened when he told her he would find a way to keep in touch, to remind her of his love for her, despite his newly made vows to his wife. He would plant a garden for them both, his wife and his mother, when he wasn't at sea so that he would share his passion and love for plants and would collect more from across the globe when he continued his travels. Their gardens would be identical, but his mother would watch the flowers grow instead of him, and her grandchildren if he was so blessed.

As the conversation faded away, Tom opened his eyes again, to see the man he had heard earlier, dressed as a sea captain, with his arms holding his mother tight within them. The Captain stared straight at Tom with a knowing smile.

Tom smiled back, now knowing what the connection was between this old garden and Rose's. Why they were almost identical and why he wanted to restore the garden using these plants. The old, neglected garden that Rose inherited along with the house would be beautiful once more and she would be thrilled.

He pictured Rose's smiling face and couldn't help but plaster a big, stupid grin on his own face. Tom was so caught up in his daydream that he didn't hear the wood splintering, or the loud crack as the large limb of the old tree fell on him.

The clock continued to chime the hour back at the Captain's

house. There was nothing amiss in this garden, but when it stopped chiming and as the silence descended, the clock tipped to an ungainly angle again. In the old garden, Tom was spread out under the weight of the heavy tree branch in an ungainly manner all of his own.

Suddenly Rose felt cold and terribly lonely. She grabbed a blanket from the end of the sofa, pulling it around her before curling up again. She slept there that night and woke up stiff and sore with Mowzer beside her. The windows were wide open, and the smell of the sea pervaded the room. Her eyes searched for the Captain's hat when she smelt the sea in the air and spotted it perched atop the mantelpiece. She reached for her phone and checked it for messages; there were a couple from Steve, but nothing from Tom. Nothing at all.

Rose left several messages for Tom over the next few days and on receiving no replies to her texting and voicemails, she phoned Tom's brother Joe on Monday morning. He hadn't seen Tom over the weekend either but told her he thought Tom was going to pop home to surprise his parents on the Friday evening, as he hadn't seen that much of them the last time, as he got so tied up with the old garden. Tom felt guilty. He was going to make it up to them and take them out to dinner. It was all a bit spur of the moment for Tom, Joe admitted. He promised to call his parents and find out what Tom was up to. It wasn't like him not to call.

Joe was a busy man with a restaurant to run, so Rose wasn't that worried when he didn't call her back straight away. She started to worry when Joe turned up on her doorstep with Tilly at his side, at a time when she knew the restaurant would be heaving with customers for his popular Monday taster menu.

Joe couldn't meet her eyes and it was Tilly that leant forward and hugged Rose hard. Joe stumbled over the words and just couldn't get the words out. Tilly whispered into Rose's ear, "They have found

Tom, Rose. He has had an accident."

Rose pushed Tilly away and grabbed her keys from the hook by the back door. "Where is he? Can I see him? What's happened?"

Tilly carefully extracted the keys from Rose's hand and led her to the sofa in the next room, while Joe put the kettle on for a cup of tea, the British cure for all ills!

Tilly sat beside her. "Rose, my dear. There is no need to go anywhere, you stay here. Tom has gone." Tilly had tried hard to keep the tears at bay, but she was failing miserably now. She turned away from Rose as they rolled down her face.

"Where has Tom gone? Why are you so upset? Has he dumped me for another garden again? I will have words with him when he gets home."

A sob caught in Tilly's throat and made her cough.

"I'll get you some water to soothe that dry cough. Wait, Tilly, you are crying? What?" As Rose reached the kitchen, she saw Joe letting Steve in. Steve looked pale and tearful as well.

"What's up with the lot of you? Tell me about Tom. I don't understand." She refused the sweet tea that Joe offered her and pulled Steve into the front room, so they could be alone.

When Rose looked at the clock, she remembered the sound of the splintering wood and the dull thud. The chiming and the silence.

"Oh, Steve, Tom has had an accident, I heard it all." Her mind raced and turned somersaults as her stomach did the same. Holding her tummy, she spun on the spot and saw the old beech tree through the window. Its roots exposed and the big void that it had left in the garden. Her beech tree fell in the winter, that made sense. It was the summer; these things didn't happen in the summer, or did they? She thought hard and remembered a conversation that she and Tom had while debating what to do with the old beech tree. Something about trees suddenly losing their branches in the summer months. She wasn't really listening to Tom when he was explaining it all, she was scrolling on her phone to find a picture of an upturned tree trunk with its roots in the air. The topic of conversation had changed and not returned to trees falling, as Tom had laughed himself silly at the thought of an upside-down tree planted with flowers in the exposed roots. Too trendy for him, he was old fashioned at heart, was her Tom.

She gasped in horror, as Steve quietly whispered in her ear and told her about Tom's accident and that a large limb of a beech tree had fallen on him in the garden he had cleared recently. He was killed instantly, but they hadn't found him until this morning when the mechanical diggers were due to move in, and the gates of the old manor house were unlocked.

Chapter Fifty-Four

Rose sent everyone away when the news had sunk in. She wanted to be alone with her thoughts. She didn't want to be fussed over. She saw Tom every time she looked at Joe, as the brothers were very alike. She needed space.

Steve ignored her at first and made himself scarce in the house. He made a lot of calls, letting her close friends and family know. The benefit of living in a small community in the countryside, just outside the main village, was that everyone looked after each other. They pulled together when it mattered. Rose hadn't been born in the village and had not been there for very long at all really. She was a very long way from being called a 'local', but she had made lots of very good friends.

Steve knew that she wouldn't call them, so she needed him to call them for her, to let them know that she was hurting and needed them. She didn't need them all together, so it was taking every ounce of him to persuade them to call another day, not turn up en masse because they were keen to let her know that they were there for her.

Everyone he talked to was shocked to the core, as he was. They couldn't believe it. Tom was in the prime of his life, fit and healthy. Rose and Tom had a lifetime to look forward to. Life was unfair.

Steve hadn't wished Tom ill, but he had wished hard for him to go away and let him look after Rose. Steve felt terribly guilty for thinking such a thing. They both cared for Rose in different ways. Tom had a way with her from the start. He seemed to know what she wanted and gave it to her before she realised it. Tom made her feel safe and happy.

He heard Rose sobbing and hovered at the doorway debating whether to go in and comfort her, but he turned away and headed for his van, which he had parked close to the house. He opened the windows wide and sat back to listen, watch and wait. He would be there for Rose and abide by her wishes. She was alone but he was not too far away, if she needed him. He would always be there for his Rose.

Rose, drained by crying slept fitfully that night. Steve kept watch outside and didn't sleep a wink in the hours of darkness. The house was too quiet. The night was too black. Nothing stirred.

As the sun rose Steve slept on soundly, exhausted with his efforts to keep watch on Rose and the house on his own all night. He was startled when someone rapped on the windscreen and yelled a 'hello'.

Val peered into the van, as Steve rubbed the sleep out of his eyes and unlocked the door. As she climbed into the passenger seat, she gently pushed his legs off so she could sit down. She passed Steve a flask full of coffee.

"You drink that to wake yourself up then we should both go and check on Rose. Make sure she is OK. Was she in the house all alone last night? Was that wise, Steve?"

"I don't know whether it was wise or not, but she looked totally shattered and I just sensed that she wanted some time on her own to process the news. It was so unexpected and has thrown us all for six. I just can't believe that we won't see him again in the garden, pottering about. I hoped that I could steal Rose from him eventually if I played the long game. He is not here to steal her from now. It doesn't seem fair, does it? So bloody not fair, Val."

Val held him tight as he sobbed into her arms like a little boy. She stroked his hair and let him cry it out. She knew he needed to get it out of his system, as she had last night when he called to tell her the news. Remembering her little Tom, he always affectionately called her 'Auntie Val', even though she wasn't a real auntie. It was his name for her, ever since he was little and holidayed by the coast with his parents and his brother, Joe.

Val hadn't been able to call it. She never quite knew which man Rose was going to end up with. Would it have been Steve or Tom? Steve had always been there for Rose on a practical level, and she knew he had held a torch for her since he first picked her up while she was staying in her annexe as the house was being fixed up.

Tom was Rose's big passion, the man had swept her off her feet, from the first time she had seen him. Rose confided in Val that he had even stayed the night there after their very first date. She confessed to Val, that she had never let a man sleep with her after a first date, but Tom was different. It just happened as if it was meant to be. Tom belonged to the house and his beloved garden, but she wondered if he ever truly loved Rose. If Rose had wanted to move, would Tom have continued to go out with Rose, or would he have bought the house and garden from her and wished her well?

They would never know for sure now, as he was gone. Leaving behind a yard full of plants and Rose all alone without him.

They were both silent as they sipped from the plastic coffee mugs that Val had twisted off the top of the flask. The house was quiet, and the bedroom curtains and shutters were not open, it looked as if Rose was still in bed.

Val and Steve watched as two magpies waddled their way across the sill of the bedroom window, one following the other. Each of them taking it in turns to rap the windowpane with their beak. Then they took flight and circled lazily around the house. One after the other. The magpies were keeping a watch of their own.

Chapter Fifty-Five

Val and Steve watched and waited with the magpies for Rose to stir, but it was nearly midday when they decided to check how she was coping. Val reasoned that Rose must be getting hungry by now and it wasn't good for her to stay in bed all day. Both Steve and Val had a key. Steve as he was always in and out since Rose had first inherited the house. He had renovated the place to a habitable standard for Rose to move in and then continued the ongoing renovations when she started to live in the property.

Val still had a key to the house from when Rose had to visit Mickey in hospital that night after he had a fall while walking at the folly. She had held onto it in case of emergencies. Val was pretty sure this was one of those times, so she knocked on the front door several times, shouted through the letterbox and on getting no answer, she unlocked the door and strode right in.

The house was empty. The bed hadn't been slept in and there was no sign of Mowzer either. Steve and Val were worried. Steve had seen Rose at the window and watched the house from his van. He knew Rose hadn't gone anywhere, but that didn't explain where she was or why Mowzer hadn't performed his usual antics when his belly was empty.

Unbeknown to Steve, Rose had crept out of the back window, dropping softly into the long grass and had sat next to the river most of the night wrapped up in several blankets against the chill of the night air. The house was so close to the water that it looked as if it was floating from several angles in the back rooms. There was a small strip of grass separating the house from the river. It was so small that the river was often mistaken for a moat. Rose sat with her back to the house looking out across to the folly at the footpath. The footpath where her mystery man had waved to her in greeting when she first set foot in the old house. The wave that had seemed so familiar and friendly. The footpath where her good friend, Mickey, who had become a father figure to her, walked daily with his devoted canine companion, Bert. The footpath to the old folly, which was connected to the house in all sorts of strange ways. The place where the womenfolk of the house looked for their men across the ocean. The place where Mickey grieved for his late wife, Iris and for the children they couldn't have but dearly wished for. Rose sat, dozing for some of the time, but when she was awake, she kept reminiscing and pining for the man she loved, had loved and wanted back so very badly.

She didn't know that Steve was sat in his van watching the house all night. She felt that she was all alone in the world and would be forever, ending up like her great aunt alone in the house, with its ethereal past. Had she known she would have been reassured, she should have realised that Steve wouldn't and couldn't have left her and was looking out for any sign of distress, ready to rush to her side the moment she needed him. Steve was waiting for a sign, any sign.

During the early hours of the night, she had considered throwing herself into the water and letting it flow over her, taking her breath and life with it. The water wasn't deep enough but she desperately wanted to try, that way they could stay together, in her house forever. Instead, of doing something so rash, the sound of the flowing water eased her. The soft notes of the running water lulled her and pulled her into its embrace. Rose hadn't wanted to sleep but as the morning light grew stronger, she fell into a deep sleep and was still fast asleep when Val and Steve called for her.

Steve and Val didn't notice that the back window was just resting on its latch. That the window was ever so slightly ajar. They raced up the footpath towards the folly, thinking that maybe Rose had slipped out and made her way up there. When they were adjacent to the house on the opposite side of the river, they saw Mickey sat down on the ground at the side of the footpath with Bert at his side. As they walked to meet him, they looked back at the house and saw why Mickey was perched where he was and why Bert was sitting so patiently at his side instead of racing around like he normally did on his walks.

Mickey had spotted a sleeping Rose and was keeping an eye on her. He had been sat there all morning and would have a bit of trouble getting up. When Steve was alongside Mickey he said, "So you were keeping an eye on her from over here, did you spot her on your morning walk? I was in my van. I had no idea she would clamber out of the window. What was she thinking?" Mickey grabbed Steve's proffered hand and stood up slowly, his bones creaking in protest.

"She has been fast asleep since I got here. I didn't like to take my eyes off her. I heard you both yelling enough to wake the dead earlier. Oh, I didn't mean the 'waking the dead' bit, how bloody insensitive. Just a bit off my game, well we all are, aren't we? What are we going to do about Rose? We can't leave her there for much longer, let's get her in and tucked up in bed or on the sofa the other side of that wall. All safe and sound."

Mickey slipped Bert on the lead when he pulled towards the river, to stop him wading across and waking Rose with a flurry of water and muddy paws. Then he and Val walked back down the path back towards the house, leaving Steve to keep watch. Bert didn't want to be pulled in what he contrived to be the wrong direction, so he started to bark.

His barking woke Rose, who sleepily looked across the water and over to the footpath. She looked across while still groggy from sleep and saw a familiar figure. Was it her Tom and it had all been a terrible dream? The figure waved at her in greeting, she waved back with a grin. Even when she realised that it wasn't Tom, it was Steve waving at her, her grin stayed there. Was her mind playing tricks? Was it Steve all along that she saw on the footpath or was it Tom? Her sleep-befuddled mind couldn't process the information, she had no chance of making sense of it, but that didn't stop her trying as tears started to fall.

Chapter Fifty-Six

Rose was cocooned by all her friends and family. She wasn't left alone again, even during the night-time. Someone was always there, maybe not at her side all the time, but in the house or in the garden, close enough to be there if she needed them.

Steve tended to the plants and garden for her, as she retreated into herself. He knew what Tom had planned and how he worked. Rose wandered aimlessly about the house and garden, starting jobs and never finishing them. Every time she entered the kitchen, she started to make a drink or a meal, getting out a mug, glass or plate. But she didn't eat or drink anything, she just ambled out of the kitchen to somewhere else instead, leaving the mound of clean crockery to grow and grow. Until someone put it all back into the pantry or put some food on the empty plates for her to eat, or a hot beverage in the mug for her to drink.

Joe came over one afternoon to sort out Tom's work stuff in the outbuildings. He arranged to meet with Steve as they shared the space. Tom's laptop contained all the business details, his tax, his customers, his contacts but his paperwork, notebooks and Post-it notes contained the essence of him. Rose had always teased him for being an old-fashioned guy at heart and he was. He preferred paper and ink, to computers and spreadsheets. He would still be handwriting his invoices with a carbon sheet if Steve hadn't taken him in hand and brought his business practices into the modern world.

When Steve sat down and tucked his long legs underneath the desk his foot made contact with something solid. When he looked to see what it was, he came out holding a ladies' shoe, just the one. It wasn't like anything Steve had ever seen Rose wear and why would she have worn a high-heeled shoe into his office? Steve held the shoe and wondered what he would say to Joe who was perched atop the desk, surrounded by paperwork going back months if not years stacked up in piles across the desk.

He came out, brandishing the shoe at Joe with a bemused grin on his face. He was still holding the shoe when Rose bustled in, all of a fluster.

"Oh, it's you, I heard people in here and a man talking. I thought you were Tom and that he was back. It's only you."

She looked at the shoe that Steve was holding and blushed. "Oh my, where did you find that? That is one of my 'going out' shoes."

Steve grinned. "Oh, it's yours Rose, is it? Phew, it would have been awkward if it was someone else's, eh! What is it doing here? Why is there just the one?"

For the first time since she had lost Tom, Rose giggled and continued to blush. The giggles erupted into gales of laughter until she held her tummy. "Put that shoe down, Steve, my tummy hurts from laughing. Oh…" The giggles subsided until she caught his eye again then she laughed until she started to cry with laughter.

The guys joined in and laughed with her, pleased to see her show a happy emotion instead of the incessant sadness that had followed her around since Tom passed. She cradled the shoe close to her as she left the men to the business stuff and went back to the house feeling suddenly ravenous. Her mood had broken for a while, and it felt good.

It took Steve and Joe the rest of the day to make a dent in the chaos of paperwork that related to Tom's gardening business. Steve had extracted all the other stuff that related to the house and his passion for roses and the old plants he loved. He popped it all into an old wooden crate Tom had under his desk and used as a footrest.

Joe had taken everything else home with him to Tom's flat over his restaurant, ready to sort out with everything else after the funeral, leaving Steve all alone in the little office. It looked bare without all Tom's gardening clutter, with the essence of all he was cleared away and tidied up. Steve sat in Tom's chair, leaning back and put his feet on his desk, feeling slightly disrespectful as he did so. He knew that Tom was always doing this when he wanted to think, so knew he wouldn't mind, he wasn't here after all. It was then that the loss hit him. He hadn't always liked the guy, he was always the competition, but they were just starting to trust each other.

It would be up to him to look after Rose now. He couldn't help but wonder how Tom would have felt about that, if he lost Rose to him. If his gardening had taken him away for long enough periods for Rose to get used to being without him. If the garden was finished and there was nothing to do, would Tom have moved on to the next big project, the next girl even!

"I promise I will look after your Rose for you. I will take care of her, if she wants me to, mind. Oh, mate, you didn't deserve to go like that, did you?" Steve talked to the silence. He had to make it right even though Tom wasn't there to reason with, to talk to. He had to say it, in the place where Tom would always be, right here, sighing and moaning about the boring side of the business, wanting to get his hands on the plants, in the dirt, making it all grow.

He talked to Tom without thinking, without reasoning that he wasn't there anymore. He was surprised when he felt a friendly shove on his shoulder, the way Tom used to do when Steve teased him. He knew it couldn't have been Tom, just his imagination working overtime and his emotions getting the better of him, but it made him feel better about it all.

It couldn't have been Tom, he reasoned, as he crossed the yard with the crate of all the paperwork that belonged to the house and related to the garden to give to Rose, could it?

Chapter Fifty-Seven

When Rose lost Tom, she anticipated that the women of the house would comfort her, her new ghostly companions would be at her side constantly, but she was to learn that the ghosts of the past had their own plans and were not predictable. She didn't need the companionship of the past, for she had people in the present who were there for her, she was not left alone.

What she didn't know was, as she and her friends slept, the house kept her safe within it. The gardens emitted a milky glow and the hedges knitted together as one. The big old manor house was connected to her house once more. Her existing dwelling moulded into the wing of the old house as it once was. There was a hush that infused the air around the land and the whole house embraced her. The women had not left her as she supposed; they were there but were not making their presence felt, as it wasn't needed.

The lady who cradled Rose so tenderly that afternoon was still right there, watching over her. Their subtle signs were understood, and Rose understood more of the history of the house. The smoke still lingered on the air in the hours of darkness as the devasting house fire remained a mystery to Rose, but the house was slowly giving up its secrets and making her its own. The handkerchief the lady had given Rose was being used to mop her own tears, now she had grief of her own to deal with. The women were used to being on their own in the house waiting for their Captains, their loves, to return.

Not all of the women had their men return; some were lost forever. As Tom was to Rose. The old handkerchief was an unexpected comfort to Rose. She couldn't help but miss the ghostly lady who had given it to her.

Rose stood on both sides of the bricked-up doorway, the house side and the garden side, at odd times during the day, willing the door to open to the past for her. For her to see Tom working in the garden again. The house only shared its secrets at a time of its own making and not on her terms. Rose wandered aimlessly around the property, searching for the ghosts of the distant past and ghosts of her present that had left her, Tom.

Mowzer slept during the day but prowled around at night. As a kitten he used to curl up in the Captain's hat, but as he grew into a big old tomcat, he didn't fit. He slept on one of Tom's old work shirts at the end of the bed during the day and during the night Rose slept in the shirt instead of her PJs, as it smelt of him and as she fell asleep, she could visualise his arms around her.

Mowzer was not alone in his nocturnal travels around the property, he was accompanied by his ghostly friends. He came home every morning smelling of pipe tobacco and of the sea. These smells mixed with those of Tom in the fibres of his work shirt and gave comfort to Rose as she slept.

When the daylight pushed the dark away in the mornings, the impregnable living barrier parted, and the garden was as it was the day before. Or was it? The garden was well tended, and the lawn never needed to be cut, the roses deadheaded.

The plants that were in the yard, were slowly being planted into the garden, one at a time, so no one noticed. The garden was looking fantastic, as it would have in the days of the bigger manor house. The changes were slight, barely perceptible. Everyone thought everyone else was doing the work, but no one was. The garden was taking shape seemingly by itself, or was it?

Chapter Fifty-Eight

Rose attended Tom's funeral by herself. Everyone had wanted to go with her, but she wanted to go alone. She had something she wanted to do on the way and didn't want anyone to know. She went to see the old garden where Tom had met his untimely end. She needed to see it for herself. She had broached the subject many times, with so many different people and they all said the same thing. That it wouldn't serve any purpose and would only upset her more. She didn't need to see the tree and what would be left of the garden for the foundations were already underway for the housing estate that was being built.

She needed to see the tree, which the local newspaper in a recent article was calling a 'widow maker'. She had to see where Tom had lost his life. She was told that he was not being careless, that trees often lose a limb in the summer months and deep down she knew that, but she needed to look, however stupid it was perceived to her friends and family.

It was only her and Val that were going to the funeral. Everyone else that wasn't family was staying away, as it was taking place near his parents' place and not where Tom and Joe had made their home. Rose had never met Tom's parents. Val had told her they were quite a formidable couple, and they wanted their boy close. His mum didn't influence his decision to live a distance away when he was alive but was asserting her will now. Rose was just his girlfriend, they weren't engaged to be married, so she had no say at all. Rose wouldn't have wanted a say; she had her memories and the little bits that Tom had left at the house and all his wonderful plants and garden ideas. She was happy with that.

Rose knew his friends were raising a glass to him at Joe's restaurant, which was closed for the day, but open to Tom's friends to pay their respects. Joe was at the funeral of his brother, but his staff were happy to do their bit. She wished she could be there instead, but it was fitting and proper that she was at his funeral, proving to his parents and his family that she had and did love him.

She peered through the locked wrought-iron gates and wondered why no one was working even though it was a weekday. Then she saw the note tied to the gate. 'This site is closed today as a mark of respect for the man who tragically lost his life'. Holding back the tears, she looked through. It was a sea of mud, but off to one side was an old beech tree, much older than the beech tree that had stood in her garden. The tree was the only living thing that she could see, for nothing else remained in what was once a beautiful garden. All traces of the old house had been erased as if it had never been there.

She wanted to feel Tom here, as it was the place he last took a breath, but nothing remained of him here. He would have hated it, the mud, the carnage and the lack of anything living as far as the eye could see. She knew it was a waste of time and her friends had been so right. If Tom was anywhere, it would be in a garden, amongst the roses that he loved best, not on a building site.

Rose did her duty at the funeral and came straight home as soon as was polite to do so after making a quick detour to his wake. She met his parents and shared her memories of Tom with them, alongside Val who stayed at her side for the duration of the funeral. She sat in her garden for a while then went to join everyone else at 'their' wake at the restaurant. This wake was not the sombre affair of the funeral and wake at his parents' house. By contrast it was a jolly affair, there was music. Joe had made a mix of all Tom's favourite bands and tracks. The conversation was loud with laughter sprinkled throughout.

Rose thought of it as a riotous party and how much Tom would have loved it. Tilly and Harriet had decorated all the tables with freshly cut flowers and lots of big, blousy roses. There were prints of the countryside, botanical art and floral jewellery all displayed with a stunning collection of photographs of the gardens where Tom had worked. Some containing a glimpse of Tom himself in the places he loved best. Looking around she noticed all the businesses that worked out of her outbuildings were there. The tributes were from his friends. With tears in her eyes she sat down surrounded by his favourite flowers and his friends. Just as everyone was set to go home, later on, Rose was joined by Val who had done her official duty, as had Rose that day, and had come to pay her respects at the 'unofficial' wake.

When everyone left, it was just Rose and Steve at the restaurant surrounded by the displays of love and affection that people had brought. Joe's staff busied themselves tidying up, so there was nothing really to do.

"Rose, we need to gather all this up and take it home for you," Steve said.

"Surely, this all belongs to Joe. He's his brother, this is his restaurant, and this was his idea after all."

"Not at all, Rose. Your friends brought all this for you. It was all meant for you. Our way of letting you know we care." Steve didn't check his emotions as he should and added, "As I will always care for you and love you, Rose."

Rose kissed him gently on his cheek. "I love you, Steve. I think I have always loved you, not in the same way as I did my Tom. He was different, in a way I can't describe. He just belonged. You are different too. You have never left my side since I first looked at the house. You…" Her words drifted off as she kissed him again.

Chapter Fifty-Nine

When Rose awoke the next day, she recalled the kisses that had stirred her so deeply that she slept without waking for the first time since she lost Tom. Steve was the perfect gentleman, in stark contrast to Tom who had jumped into bed with her when the first opportunity presented itself, which was after their very first date. The date took place in the evening of the very first day they met. Incredulous, really, as that had been entirely out of character for Rose. There was always something about Tom that entranced her. He had belonged to her, and she was taking back what was hers.

Steve, on the other hand, had been special from the start. He had been at her side ever since she made the decision to keep the house she inherited. He had patiently explained how to renovate such an old property, dealt with all the official requirements for her, managing and budgeting carefully so she could afford to do so. She had hired him the day she met him, not bothering to get anyone else to quote on the work. She had always trusted him implicitly. He was honest through and through.

She always thought him a little boring, compared to her flamboyant Tom. Tom was a true character, people remembered him, loved him and admired his passion for his work. Steve was solid, dependable but not boring when you got to know him. He just took his time with things and taking his time with Rose, had enabled Tom to sneak in and get the girl!

Steve had gently admonished her when she kissed him, stepping aside to stop her and himself from getting carried away. Rose felt an embarrassed blush engulf her when she realised what she had done. Not knowing how she would ever face Steve again, she snuggled back under the covers and drifted off to sleep.

Out in the yard, trying not to make too much noise were most of the people that were at the restaurant the day before. When the drinks flowed, so did the ideas of how to 'manage' for the foreseeable future. They had all agreed they needed to move all the plants that were still sat in the yard, where Tom had left them ready to plant. They were going to move all the pots across to the bottom of the garden next to what remained of the uprooted beech tree. They would get them out of the yard, so Rose would not be reminded of Tom and his plans for the garden every time she stepped out of her back door. They all supposed that they would not be there for long, as they suspected Rose would make headway on the garden to honour Tom's memory. They all wanted to help her but wanted her to rest and grieve properly first.

The work was conducted in near silence, as the majority of them were nursing sore heads from the night before. Steve was conspicuous in his absence. When the last of the heavy pots were wheeled through the garden to their temporary site on the rickety old wheelbarrow that Mickey found resting against the wall, Tilly wailed, "Oh, bloody hell, there is some distance to water this lot. Didn't anyone notice that Tom had them lined up next to the outside tap? We have created an extra job for Rose!"

Nodding at Tilly, Mickey retorted quick as a flash, "That's right, my dear. Let's keep the girl busy. No point sitting around feeling sad. As she walks through the garden with the watering cans or if she is sensible, with this wheelbarrow with the watering cans atop, she will remember Tom. She will look at the plants she is watering, maybe glance at the labels. In the evening she will look up the plants she is unfamiliar with, look for the old planting plans. This little detour twice a day, will give her purpose. That's my grand plan. Otherwise, it will fall to me and Val who live close by."

"Oh no, Mickey, your idea, your work. Don't rope me into it!" Val retorted, waving her fist at him.

"You don't mean that. You would do anything for that girl in there, wouldn't you? And your little Tom. Remember they were his plants, you know!"

"That is so below the belt, Mickey! But you are right. Of course, I will!"

Rose watched from the window as the tired group made their way through the garden. She had heard every word. She wiped the tears from her eyes and forced a tiny smile. She was so very lucky to have friends like these. Mickey was always full of good advice, and she suspected that he had found a similar job to keep him busy when his beloved wife had passed.

Rose stepped back from the window as they passed, not wanting to make herself known. She listened waiting for a knock at the door or the sound of the back door being unlocked, but her friends respected her need for solitude and left her alone.

She sat on the edge of the bed and watched as one by one those who had arrived by car drove off. She was subconsciously watching for Steve. She didn't see him with the others and didn't see his van drive off. She hoped she hadn't upset him by kissing him the night before. It was so unlike him not to be in the thick of anything that needed repair whether that was in her house or on her land.

She didn't regret kissing him after he told her that he cared for her and loved her. Had she unwittingly loved two men at the same time?

She knew that her ghostly Captain approved of Tom as she had seen them sat side by side on the bench. What would the Captain make of Steve? Or had he already given his seal of approval by the way Steve was accepted into the very fabric of the place, and that the house had revealed some of its secrets to him? It was Steve who had found the figurehead hidden in the loft space after all. The roof had been patched up over the years, but no one else had seen the package tucked away right under the sloping roof timbers.

Chapter Sixty

Rose had expected the atmosphere of the house to change now that Tom was no longer sharing the space with her; she felt that the house would grieve the same way that she was. The turmoil of the ticking clock had signified what was to come and now the event had come to pass, the house seemed at peace.

Rose sat with the tin box she had found buried under the beech tree on her lap. She wanted to share the sadness of the lady that had buried it. This was her way of seeking comfort with the past womenfolk of the house. When she looked closer at the silver brooch, she noticed that the back didn't seem to fit and it was jutting out from the edge ever so slightly. She prised the two edges apart to reveal two locks of hair that had been woven together in a plait in the shape of a heart. It was a mourning brooch. She cradled it in both hands, the brooch no bigger than a matchbox. Small, delicate and priceless. No diamonds but the very essence of the two people that lived and loved.

What was contained within the brooch was too precious to be exposed to the air for long, so she snapped it together and instead of putting it back into the box put it in the pocket of her trousers. She did the same thing with the pocket watch, examining it carefully and checking for any hidden compartments. The watch was worn, and the patina was smooth. She stroked the watch and held it to her ear. It had stopped, the hands fixed. It rattled when she shook it. There was something adrift inside. She stuffed it into the other pocket of her trousers, disinclined to put it back in the box.

Subconsciously she was invoking the spirts of the house to make themselves known to her, to share her grief. In reality it doesn't work like it does in the movies and the best-selling novels. It all happens for a reason and at the right time. It was not that time, however much Rose wanted it to be.

The brooch and watch were forgotten in her pockets when she got up and stopped feeling sorry for herself. When she wasn't watching and waiting, subtle changes started to happen around her. An audience wasn't required, it would play out without a prompt, and so it did.

As Rose wandered from room to room not quite knowing what to do with herself, if she had looked around, she would have noticed that she was not as alone as she thought she was.

For just behind her, a ghostly friend was back, about two steps away, peering over her shoulder. As she walked across the front room to gaze across the garden to where the old beech tree once stood, the neat black boots and the long white skirt, edged in pink, could be seen following behind her.

When she looked out at the back of the house, she leant against the figurehead set at the window, constantly keeping watch. The head tipped slightly to one side and rested on top of Rose's in a silent embrace.

Another figure of a lady watched over her from the top of the tower. Below the folly, the bench was bowed with the weight of a Captain sitting silently surveying his land.

It was in the garden that she was never alone. The smell of pipe smoke wafted in the air whenever she stepped outside. The heavy tread of a man behind her.

As always, her faithful feline trotted alongside her, tail aloft. Head held high, watching over his mistress.

Mowzer saw the stranger first, when he parked his battered Mini in the lane alongside the house. The cat was usually a good judge of character, but he didn't know what to make of the man. He was tall, lanky with round, horn-rimmed glasses balanced at the end of his nose. As he walked, he peered through the thick lenses, tilting his head to the floor in order to see. It made him walk with a stoop. He carried a brown leather briefcase and would have looked imposing if he drew himself up to full height. Rose didn't notice him, but Mowzer did. He stared unblinkingly at the stranger and set his paws square, sizing him up like a large mouse that he wanted for his supper. Mowzer had grown into a very large tomcat and was the size of a small dog.

The man took no notice of the menacing cat and almost knocked him over with his briefcase as he set it down on the floor and put his hand out to shake Rose's and introduce himself.

Rose was watering the plants in the part of the garden she had named 'Tom's patch'. She was hot, sweaty and very grimy when she took his hand in hers and shook it politely.

"I was not expecting anyone today. Whatever it is you are selling, I am really not interested, would you mind leaving the way you came? Thank you!" Rose nibbled her lower lip to stop herself adding a rude remark.

"Bless you, I am not selling anything. You are right, I should have called first, but when I heard all about you, I just had to come and see you."

Rose chewed both lips and scooped up Mowzer from the floor and pulled him close, much as a child would a teddy bear for comfort. She hated confrontation. Mowzer emitted a low, deep growl before he leapt at the man's face. The man picked up his briefcase, shielded his face with it and knocked Mowzer to the ground.

Unhurt, Mowzer scrambled to his feet and looked ready to sink his teeth and claws into his trousers.

"I am so very sorry about that. Are you OK? He has never done that before to anyone."

The man frowned and handed Rose his business card. "Most animals love me, but your cat is not a fan, is he? Please let me talk to you. If not today, let me make an appointment. What day suits you?"

Rose took his card. "Well, not today. Come back tomorrow at 11 in the morning."

The man nodded curtly and turned on his heels and strode away. "Can we meet indoors, preferably without the cat present?"

Sinking to the ground and with her arms around Mowzer, she watched him go. She tried to tuck his card into her pocket, and it didn't fit as her pockets were full. She pulled out the brooch to stuff the business card in. Thinking of the hair heart contained within, she pulled a tuft of long grass and tugged it into the shape of a heart, working in extra lengths of grass to give it substance.

It calmed her. Right there behind her sat the other woman of the house, weaving an identical grass heart. The woman was not visible to the visitor and to Rose, but Mowzer had nestled into the folds of her long skirt and when Rose turned around, he had disappeared along with her. Her grass heart was finished and lay hidden in the grass.

Chapter Sixty-One

Rose admonished herself for being daft enough to make an appointment with the odd man that Mowzer had taken such a dislike to. His business card looked above board, but she called Steve to see if he knew the man. Steve told her that he knew him as James. He was the deputy curator of a little local museum on the seafront, tucked away between an ice cream parlour and a gift shop. It catered for tourists mainly with the photographs, maps and artefacts of the local area, seashore and prominent landmarks. The local history society met there every other month and James was a bit of a local history nut. He wasn't the stereotypical curator. He was in his forties and had just returned from an unexplained trip aboard. No one knew the reason he had left so suddenly. The rumours circulating said that he had only returned when he found out that the current curator was retiring, as he desperately wanted the job. James was the local busybody and was always snooping around, but Rose had never met him as he had been abroad ever since she had lived there.

He was an odd man and not particularly well liked. He went on to say, "James was born in the wrong era. He obsesses about things that happened years ago, but doesn't seem to care about the here and now. He keeps himself to himself and apart from his elderly father and those he speaks to in his 'local history' group he has no friends, doesn't date at all..." Steve's conversation faltered.

There was a silence for a few moments, until Steve said, "Do you want me to come over and be with you when James comes to call? Do you need me?" Rose could hear the uncertainty in Steve's voice and guessed that he was giving her space to grieve and wanted her to ask him first.

Rose didn't have to think about her answer, she wanted Steve at her side and really didn't need the space Steve always felt she needed.

"Yes, of course I do, silly. You come over when you want, just let yourself in. I think we can both agree that we don't need to tiptoe around this anymore. You are my very best friend and have been since the time I first laid eyes on you. Stop staying away!" Her voice rose as her emotions started to get the better of her.

She heard Steve gulp and clear his throat and answer, "Will be there with you as soon as."

Steve and Rose greeted James formally as he knocked on the front door. This showed that he was not familiar with the house rules since Rose had lived there. Everyone who knew her came to the back door, unless it was a special occasion or Christmas. It added to the strangeness of the visit.

James pushed past Rose this time and strolled into the front room as if he owned the place. He pulled out a chair at the dining table and gestured to Rose to sit down. He opened his briefcase and in a bizarre fashion, tipped the contents out onto the table. Rose grabbed the vase to prevent it from tipping over and pushed it further back on the table as the wave of paperwork flooded the surface.

He then folded his arms and looked straight at Rose. "This is everything I have on this plot of land and the dwellings. The timeline goes back a very long way." He grabbed a printout from the bottom of the pile and pulled it towards him. The paperwork tottered on the edge of the table and Rose caught a couple of photos before they hit the floor. James snatched them from her hands and put them back on the table.

"I am in charge of this discussion with you. There is an order to what I have to tell you. Stop fiddling, girl, and listen."

Rose sat back and reached for Steve's hand underneath the table. He took her hand and held it tight, as James rolled the printout across the table. There in black and white was the timeline of the house showing everyone who had ever lived there. James's handwriting, very tiny but incredibly neat, peppered the typed document.

"Oh my god, this is incredible. Look, Steve, look, there is my great aunt and oh my goodness, look at all the Captains listed. I thought there were two, but there are more, many more."

James smiled as he lunged at the paperwork again. "Now, young lady, look at this." He produced with a flourish another document with a long list of ships. In tiny capital letters James had added where they sailed to and what they carried on each leg of the journey.

James became a different man. He took on a larger-than-life character as if he was playing a role on the stage. He continued to produce document after document, laughing as he flourished them under Rose's nose each time.

When he tossed a pile of old photographs into the air. His excitement was infectious, making Rose giggle. She was amazed to see what disregard he had for such old things, which surely should have been handled with much more care.

It was the weirdest meeting that Rose had ever had. The man was acting like a magician and not a deputy curator. His showmanship was exquisite.

Continuing to giggle, Rose sorted through the photos and portraits of her Captains, his ladies and his crew. Horses, carriages, dogs, cats and exotic birds too. The faces were so familiar to her.

When she noticed that one portrait showed the Captain wearing his hat, she left the table and ran into the back room to retrieve her own Captain's hat from the mantelpiece.

She brought it back to James and Steve. They were discussing how strange it was that the portrait was not altogether more formal. The hat should be straight and square on his head. It was then that they all noticed that he looked as if he was about to join in their laughter. His smile was wide. His eyes twinkling. A jolly old Captain indeed. Rose loved this little portrait of her Captain. It was informal and charming. She so wanted it.

James noticed that she was holding the portrait tighter. "Hey there, girl, you need to give that back to me," he demanded.

Rose stopped grinning and started to wonder how James had managed to get his hands on everything he had pulled from his briefcase. It was all connected to her and her family. What was this James doing with it all?

Chapter Sixty-Two

The fun had evaporated, and the smiles and laughter were gone. James looked crestfallen at the change and in an attempt to hide his discomfort he started to tidy up the mound of paperwork. He tidied up the photographs into one pile, the portraits and sketches in another. All his printouts and notes in another and what looked like a family tree on the top.

Rose stared at the family tree and snatched it from the top of the pile. She ignored the look that James gave her and scanned the document from top to bottom. It was all laid out in front of her, the only person that was missing was her. She searched for James's name, hoping that he wasn't part of her distant family. She didn't want to be related to him.

The friendly vibes had ebbed away fast. Steve was glaring across at James, warning him not to push his luck and let Rose look. James was at a loss at what to do.

"Rose, what are you looking for and where has your smile gone? I haven't missed anyone from the tree. This is my best work. I have had an interest is this old house and land for as long as I can remember. I have loved researching it and hunting for identities of all the supposed ghosts that live here. There is no such thing as ghosts, just history and people's vivid imaginations. I believe that sometimes the past leaves an impression on its surroundings and there it can be replayed. Like setting up a recording to watch again. No ghosts though, unless you have had one too many!" He mimed a drink action with his hand and laughed nervously. He pushed his hair from his eyes and attempted to push his glasses back up and over the bridge of his nose.

"I didn't want you to have it now, but I wanted to ask you if I could display it all at the museum. The Captain's house is part of the rich heritage of the area and the captains deserve to be remembered and understood. Would you work with me, to get the essence of the place onto the display?"

Rose sat back in her chair and looked out of the window into the garden to regain her equilibrium before answering. The guy was certainly odd. She was so relieved that he was not listed in the family tree. The very thought of having to give up her beloved house to anyone or have them contest her aunt's will, had worried her. Ever since she inherited that house. She had always felt her good fortune and amazing inheritance was too good to be true. She wouldn't have been surprised if someone popped up out of the woodwork to scoop it away from her. Her ex-boyfriend Mike's constant scheming and jealousy had made her worrying worse.

She looked at the family tree so neatly presented, and it made it real, definite and unbreakable, the house was hers and hers alone. The worry that had plagued her for months lifted and her head felt clearer than it had for some time.

"I can't wait to tell Tom all this," she said and then bit her lip so hard she made it bleed. Steve grabbed her hand and squeezed it tightly.

"Yes, Tom would be thrilled with all this information, wouldn't he?" Steve whispered.

James took the turn of conversation as his cue to leave. He left his tidying and picked up his now empty briefcase.

"I will leave all this with you, Rose. It belongs to the house after all. I have made copies of everything for the display. I won't do anything until I hear from you. Goodbye now, I will see myself out."

Rose watched as James walked away from the house towards the lane where he had parked his car. She noticed that Mowzer was sat under the front hedge close to the old 'Captain's House' sign that she had put back in its rightful place. As James drew alongside Mowzer leapt out from the foliage and made him jump. He trotted after James like a guard dog, making sure he was off the property.

"He really doesn't like that James. I wonder why."

"I can tell you why," said Steve. "He lodges with Dale, the vet. Perhaps Mowzer can smell the vets on his clothes. Why he lodges there is mystery to everyone, as he is not known as an animal lover. Perhaps the attraction is Dale?"

Disinterested in his reply, Rose was busy looking for the portrait of her smiling Captain.

"I love this picture; do you think that James would mind if I took this out of his display? It feels so personal, and I reckon it needs to be here, over the fireplace, watching over the place. Do you think?"

Steve took it across to the wall, holding it up so Rose could see what it would look like.

"I think it needs a frame, don't you? We might have one in the outbuilding, let's look."

Arm in arm they made their way to the outbuilding, Rose holding the smiling Captain in her hands. Steve seemed to know exactly where to look and found a frame that matched the portrait perfectly.

By the evening the smiling Captain was framed and up on the wall. She had wanted a portrait of a Captain in the house since she first set eyes on it, and there he was. The front room belonged to the house again, just as she had pictured many months ago. It was unfinished but not unloved as it once was. Rose could ignore the clock that she had grown to hate standing lop sided against the wall. It brought bad memories of Tom and the odd chiming that had foretold the end of his life, that Tom's life was ticking away. Now she had the Captain as a focal point in the room, the clock was of no interest.

Steve and Rose didn't notice that the clock was slowing regaining its upright habit. It was not as wonky as it was when Tom passed. It was beginning to stand up straight again. The clock rumbled and growled as they left the room to have dinner together. The noise it made was so soft that neither of them heard it, as they strode for the second time that day arm in arm out of the door.

Chapter Sixty-Three

Over the next couple of weeks, Rose worked her way through everything that James had left on the table. One of the earlier maps showed an old manor house that was a substantial size, dominating the plot of land in a C shape, with two wings, coach house, stables and other outbuildings. The maps recorded the house reducing in size and the folly being built.

Depending on the time period, there were paintings of the house or early photographs. The photographs showed a small staff standing proudly in front of the property. House maids, cooks, gardeners. The Captain was only captured on his own, as were the women of the house, never together. Rose surmised that they must have spent long periods of time apart when he was at sea.

There wasn't much about the garden, but most of that she already knew as it was in Tom's journal. She was sure she was missing a connection somewhere. Tom was so sure that the old clock belonged in her house. His insistence that the plants from the old garden he had died in belonged here too, was too compelling to ignore. She spent hours poring over the documents, looking for some clues. When she was in the garden, she often stood in the old yew and stared back at the house, looking for more clues. Why was Tom so tied up in that old garden near his parents'? Why did he go back and sit under that old tree? It didn't make sense.

She kept asking herself why it was Steve she turned to for comfort.

Why didn't she want anyone else? Why was it him that she turned to and talked with for hours? It was because it was easy, she didn't have to make definite plans with Steve. He just pottered about the place, making himself useful and being there for her. The little jobs on the house were getting finished around her. He bypassed her with the detail, talking directly to Lisa to finish the front room instead of her. Lisa was directing him from afar and at the same time checking in on her friend on a daily basis. The wallpaper had been reprinted and the wall that Steve had finished looked absolutely stunning. Rose decided to keep the once hidden door uncovered, so Steve made good the surrounding area and ensured that the door was sound. There was no need for a 'modern feature' wall in this room. The door was definitely a feature, as was the clock. The front room was coming together.

Along with Rose, the garden was missing Tom's care too. Steve kept it neat and tidy, but he wasn't really a gardener by trade and was unwilling to mess about with it too much. That was a step too far. Rose was not ready for that, and neither was he.

They messed about in the garden together, watering and caring for the plants. Steve cut the grass and Rose trimmed the edges of the lawn. He kept Rose busy in the garden, doing his best to make sure it didn't become a chore and wasn't too painful for her to manage. He didn't want her to neglect the garden because it brought back too many memories of Tom. Steve didn't touch the new plants as he didn't have a clue where he should put them. Rose hadn't shared the garden journal with Steve for she slept with it underneath her pillow, and it was too precious.

Steve spent most of his waking hours at the house with Rose, putting his business on hold for a time, subcontracting what he could and delaying the rest. He was very popular, and his customers were by and large willing to wait for him to fit them in anyway as he was so very busy. A victim of his own success really. His customers were local and were used to him prioritising Rose and the Captain's house anyway.

Rose and Steve slipped into a cosy routine, the pair of them pottering around the house together during the day and late into the night. They usually ate dinner together and snuggled up together on the bench in the garden with a bottle of wine and something savoury to eat. As the dark fell, Steve made his excuses and made his way home. They were growing into more than just friends, but Steve was very respectful to his Rose and didn't push for anything more. He was sure that they belonged together and had done from the start. Steve was biding his time, his strategy from the beginning had been 'all good things come to those who wait'.

Rose appreciated Steve's company but was equally pleased when he went home, and she had the house to herself again. She never went straight to bed, and she stayed up till the early hours, feeling the house settle with her. The sounds of the past, hearing the heavy footsteps across the floorboards and the light skittering tread of the women too, with the comforting glow of lamplight in the windows. The doors opening and closing randomly, making a barely perceptible tap as they shut.

Sometimes she slept in a chair or curled up on the window seat at the back of the house. Upstairs the figurehead kept her company and dominated her dreams so she dreamt of the ocean, the swells of the waves, the freedom and space. She would hear her Captain call orders to his crews in all kinds of weather. Always waking, with her PJs soaked in sea spray and feeling exhilarated.

She never dreamt of Tom and as the days went by, she missed him less and less. It was Steve who included him in their conversation and seemed to miss him more, as he wanted to finish the garden as well as the house for Rose.

Chapter Sixty-Four

Rose woke to Mowzer hitting her nose with his paw. He wasn't gentle, it was a definite whack. He meant business. She had fallen asleep curled up on the window seat in the back room. There wasn't much space, so being woken in such a way resulted in her hitting the floor rather quickly and sending Mowzer flying. Being a cat, he landed on his feet and scampered to the door which was shut.

Rose wrinkled her nose as the smoke reached her. She tentatively crossed the room on all fours. Reaching for the fleecy throw on the sofa that was easy to reach from the floor, she pulled it across her mouth and stood up to open the door a crack. The air was full of black smoke, so thick she could hardly see. She shut the door, put the throw down at the bottom and ran over to the window. She opened it and clambered down onto the grass following a skittish Mowzer leading the way.

She didn't hesitate but scrambled down the bank of the river and crossed to the other side. She didn't see where Mowzer went but knew he wouldn't have followed her through the water. She got the shock of her life when the cat started to shake the water from his fur at her feet.

The grass was wet underfoot. It was chilly in her PJs, but Rose didn't notice. She was too busy staring at her beloved house burning. The house was well alight; flames were coming out of the rafters. Ignoring the wet grass, she sat down and wailed in horror. She was so caught up in the moment that she didn't look around, for there were others with her in the darkness.

Not in their PJs but in their night clothes with cloth caps on their heads, the woman wailing with her and staring across at the fire. When Rose noticed that she was not alone, she turned her attention from the fire and stared at her companions instead. They looked as if they were as real as her, but there was a shimmer, a haze surrounding them.

Perturbed, she turned back to the fire and looked carefully at the house alight in front of her on the other side of the river. Her cottage was untouched and was not burning. It was the once larger house that was ablaze, the part of the house that was no longer there in her present.

She was witnessing the terrible tragedy that had befallen the house of her ancestors. She was experiencing the fire as did the women folk at her side. Witnessing the demise of the once grand old house. She thought there was nothing she could do but watch until she felt the bump of another body at her side. She looked across and recognised her lady companion, wailing into her pink and white handkerchief and mopping her tears. She saw the men folk attempting to douse the flames, but she didn't see the Captain.

Then she saw the Captain standing right in front of her. He was shielding the women from the heat of the flames, from the terror of seeing the house burn. He held a carved wooden stick in his hands. At the top of the stick there was a dragon carved into the wood. Its eyes shining bright in the light of the fire. The dragon's eyes made with rubies, glittered and sparkled as the light grew, the fire danced and increased in intensity.

Rose was so fascinated by the dragon on his stick, its eyes drew her in. She blinked her eyes every time the stones flashed and reached out her hand to caress the dragon's head. On contact it felt real, very real. The eyes flashed again and again, until the light was constant but no longer red. It was the orange hue of the sunrise.

Rose woke on the far side of the river; she was so very cold and wet through. It was still very early, and she raced back to the house before anyone could spot her, keeping a keen eye out for Mickey on his early walk with Bert. She made it back to the house before anyone saw her and raced to run a hot shower to warm up. At the bottom of the stairs the smell of smoke hit her again and the memories of the night before assailed her.

As the hot water rained on her naked body, she remembered clambering out of the window, the fire, the woman and the Captain. Where was his stick? How and why did it seem so real? Those eyes, those red, red eyes.

After her shower, she went back to bed and dreamt once more of the Captain and his dragon stick. Something new that she hadn't seen before. There was no sign of the stick in any of the paintings she had seen, and she was sure she would have recalled something as unusual and unique as that.

Chapter Sixty-Five

It was some months before Rose put the final pieces of the puzzle together and made sense of the unusual stick, its distinct carving and those red flashing eyes. It haunted her dreams, but she rarely recollected her dreams during her waking hours.

For one simple reason, Rose was happy. Her friends worked alongside her in the outbuildings or lived close by. Her parents were in the process of moving to the neighbouring town by the sea. Mickey and Bert continued to pop in most days. She was still close to Joe, Tom's brother, but found it hard to be in his company as he reminded her of Tom, as they looked very alike.

The paintings she discovered when she first moved in were found to be originals and worth a great deal, so she didn't have to worry about money anymore. She had a steady income from the outbuildings and worked for her friends as and when they needed an extra pair of hands. She found she had a flair with flowers, could ice a cake, but her main skill was admin. She organised everyone. Keeping their schedules, making appointments and sorting their invoices. She had helped Steve out with his administrative stuff first. Unbeknown to her, Steve hadn't needed any help, he just let it pile up on purpose, so he could give it to Rose. Dotty was in on the act too, as she used to help him when it all got too much and now, she left him alone to give it all to Rose. Steve suspected that Dotty would get the admin jobs eventually, when Rose found her true skill. He suspected that she had green fingers, through and through, and would have worked this out earlier if Tom hadn't been around to do it for her.

Rose had planted out the garden herself in the last days of summer. She used Tom's journal for reference and followed it to the letter. Tom had labelled all the plants, so she knew what was what. The directions were clear in the old journal. The odd word was faded or missing, but she improvised them, and the garden was looking superb. She had kept all the labels tucked in the old journal, mixing the old with the new.

Sometimes, when she wasn't sure what to do, there was a subtle sign in the garden; she was sure Tom was pointing the way, giving her a clue.

Steve and Rose had taken it very slowly, but they were now a couple. There was no big passion, their friendship just morphed into love. It was a different kind of love, a lasting love. The type of love that connects two people long before they ever realise. Steve and Rose were alike in their thinking, and it was a natural process to be together. So natural that their friends didn't really notice it happening and neither did they. It evolved, their love bloomed as a flower in a garden. She was sure Tom would be happy that she was loved and looked after.

It was Steve who brought the carvings around the house to her attention. He leant over the banisters to ask her to bring up a towel from downstairs when there was nothing to dry himself on after taking a long soak in the bath after his long working day. Then he caught his fingers on the rough carving etched underneath.

"How long has that been there, Rose? I didn't notice it when I varnished the wood," he said as he snuggled in next to her on the sofa.

"That has always been there. There are several all around the house and over in the folly too. I reckon it is the Captain pointing the way. I always found one when I needed help with something. Tom always said that we would find treasure one day! Like the gold ring that Tom found in the garden, that I never take off. This beautiful locket and chain that is right here around my neck, that was hiding under the beech tree when I took the time to look. How crazy is that? Perhaps it was you that it was meaning after all, you do have a splinter in that finger!"

Rose kissed his finger and gazed across at the folly. Across the water she saw two glowing red spots in the dark.

She immediately thought of the Captain's stick, only seen the once when the house was burning. Maybe the Captain needed his dragon to be found in order to protect the house once more. It was his talisman, after all.

Chapter Sixty-Six

The next morning Rose searched the long grass where she had seen the red lights the evening before. The grass was undisturbed, growing long and in tufts. There was nothing amiss. Rose was bitterly disappointed, as she expected to find it just lying there in the grass, even though that was so unrealistic. If it was important to the Captain, he would not have been so careless. He would have hidden it somewhere for a reason. The location was important. She retraced her steps until she was certain she was dead opposite the back window and looked again, maybe he had buried it. She pulled at a tuft of grass with her hands, and some of it came away. She rummaged in the dirt until she found a large stone with her fingertips. Not able to leave it alone, she scrabbled around for a bit longer but made no progress at all.

With a sigh and a swift kick, she made her way back to the house for a spade to dig with. She popped into the office that Tom had shared with Steve. She had kept all his tools on his side of the office where his old desk had been. It was her way of keeping him a part of her new relationship with Steve, blending the old with the new. She used his tools regularly so was often in and out. Grabbing the spade, she ran headfirst into Steve.

Seeing her sheepish look, he grabbed her arm. "What are you up to now, Rose? I can see mischief in your eyes," he teased.

"Come with me and grab something to dig with," she cried and dashed out of the room. Feeding on her excitement, he grabbed a hoe and followed her across the yard, past the old yew tree and up the footpath to the other side of the river.

He started to dig alongside Rose and when they both hit rock, they dug around until they could free it from the impacted soil around it. It took two of them to lift the heavy rock and just as they were looking into the hole, a shadow fell across them.

"Ooh, this looks good. What you up to, kids!" cried Mickey as Bert tried to get into the recently excavated hole.

Grabbing his collar, Rose yelled, "You frightened the life out of me, Mickey. I thought it was the Captain looking over my shoulder."

"You both look so guilty, it looks as if you are digging up a body. Oh, you are not, are you?" Mickey looked anxiously at the pair of them.

"Step back, the pair of you and let me see," Rose cried. She reached into the hole and grabbed something. It was just the right size, but it was wedged in.

"This hole needs to be bigger to get it out. Here, Mickey, take this spade and dig there and I will use my hands. Steve, you work out your end!" Rose took charge and with a little more digging the hole was big enough. Rose stretched down and pulled it out.

It was uncannily untouched by the years in the ground. It should have rotted away, being made of wood, but it looked as if it was carved just the day before. There, twinkling in the sunlight, the eyes of the dragon stared back at the three of them gazing in disbelief at the stick with the head of a dragon.

"Oh my god. This is the stick that belonged to the Captain. It has been here all this time, protecting the house and everything. Look, there is the folly, the outbuildings and the house. It is in the middle. The carvings are a subtle clue, it is in the middle of a lopsided triangle."

Rose wrapped the dragon stick in her jumper and brought it back into the house. The eyes of the carved dragon shone brighter as it got closer to the house. When she leant it against the wall looking back across the water, in the same position as the figurehead in the room above, the eyes glowed bright. It belonged to the house, as did Rose.

Chapter Sixty-Seven

Since the time she was born, Rose was destined to be part of the story. When her great aunt suggested her name, she had inexplicably linked her to the house. She knew that she would leave her precious house and all she held dear to another 'Rose'. The past and the present were entwined in the Captain's land and house. The past always had a role in the future there. The captains always found a way to signpost the fortune of the house in the future. The little carvings that others would have thought just whimsical or old damage that needed to be put right, were seen by those who knew their importance. Or those that were trusted.

The little nuances of the property were barely perceptible to others, unless they had a past connection to the house or true connection with its people.

One of the first captains of the house used his skills as a navigator and captain to build a grand house for the love of his life, which eventually cost him his family and his mother. He worked hard to maintain the connections with both. He spent a lot of time at sea to improve his beloved house and bring back the new specimens of botanical wonders that his wife Rose loved. They spent lots of time apart because of his time at sea. He was a victim of his own success as a sought-after captain, a fair captain and one that was not afraid of the unknown. He spent less time with his wife than he wanted, less time with his family.

His son, the second Captain, married his very own Rose, a Dorothy Rose. This sad couple had to deal with the devasting fire that cut the house down to size. Although they lived in what was really just a cottage, without the grandeur of the past, they made the time to enjoy each other. This Captain spent his time and money on the garden and enhanced the tiny folly so his wife could look out to the ocean when he was away, sending him her love and keeping him safe.

Generation after generation, the women loved their men and cherished their home. When Rose's great aunt gifted her the house, the ghosts of the past remained. Only two Captains have made themselves known to Rose, but there have been many more. She has encountered and got to know just a few from the past generations of women who lived there. As her family had lived on the same plot of land for many, many generations, the echoes of the past would always be part of the very essence of the place.

Her great aunt had not been blessed with children of her own and lost her love, her Captain, when he drowned at sea as a young man. Her great aunt was happy at the house and rarely left it, for the women of the past kept her company when her Captain never returned to her side.

The ghostly Captains and women of the past are woven into the fabric of the house and grounds and those who love the house will always remain.

Chapter Sixty-Eight

Rose couldn't forget Tom and when she spent time in the garden, she would think of him. Now she was with Steve, she realised that she had loved Tom with a passion, but she was sure that it wouldn't have lasted. Tom loved her garden as much or perhaps even more than he did her; he belonged to the house but not to her. She didn't know how such a thing could happen. A place and not a person. How that would have worked out if Tom hadn't met his end in the other garden, they would never know. The other garden had added colour and vibrancy to her own. The garden that had practically mirrored the Captain's. But why and how did the history match?

Tom's journal had held the answers all along. She couldn't read all of the spidery handwriting and skipped over the same unreadable words time and time again. The journal was so precious to her so once she had finished with the planting and the garden was at rest for the winter, she stopped looking at it so much. She tucked it away in a drawer and wrapped it in his old work shirt. When she found it again, after some time had passed, her eyes picked out the words she had missed before.

The missing word was 'mother'. Why would the gardener be referring to his mother? It didn't make sense until she read it again. Could it be the Captain's mother? There were two of everything listed, one for her garden and one for his mother's garden. That made sense. The gardens were made at the same time and were practically identical.

It didn't explain how Tom fitted in, but in its own unique way the house did. Little by little, bit by bit. Unbeknown to Rose, Tom came from a line of gardeners that had tended the Captain's childhood home and then the Captain's own home in Kent. He was as closely entwined to the garden as she was to the house.

Sometimes, she glimpsed Tom from the corner of her eye as a young boy playing amongst the flowers. Other times she spotted the man she remembered and loved watching her wistfully while tending to his roses. Tom had got his wish to be with his beloved garden for eternity. For the Captains would always share the house with those they loved.

Rose was often compelled to make her way to the back of the house and look out of the window. Her eyes would look across the river to the land beyond. She often caught sight of a man walking along the footpath to the rear of the house. He always looked across and would see her at the window. Then he would stop, wave a hand in greeting and walk on, only to stop and wave again.

She could never quite make out his face, but she always wondered if it was Tom waving at her.

Was it Tom she saw that day when she first came to the house, who had waved at her from the footpath? Or was it the ghostly form of Tom that she was so used to catching a glimpse of now.

Would she ever know?

CAPTAINS AND ROSES

Captain (1794-1806)

Captain Nathaniel PETTS (1865-1948)
Married **Rose** (1870-1946)
Her sister, **Violet** *(Born 1880) is Rose's Great Great Grandmother*

Captain Albert PETTS (1900-1970)
Married Dorothy **Rose** (1901-1978) *who had a daughter -* **Lily Anne Rose Born 1930**

Captain (Born 1928 – Lost at Sea)
Married Lily Anne **Rose** (1930-2017)
the daughter of Dorothy Rose and her captain

No children as captain lost at sea.

Lily Anne Rose left 'The Captain's House' to Rose

ABOUT THE AUTHOR

Mel J Wallis lives in Kent and has based her Captain trilogy in the Kent county. She lives in a village on the North Downs with her husband, Andy and two teenage daughters, Amy and Louise. She shares her home with the family's two cats, Pickle and Kitty and the garden with their elderly rabbit, Apple.

She enjoys walking the Kent countryside deep in thought, contemplating her plotlines and developing her characters. In the summer you will find her stretched out in the sunshine in her garden and in the winter curled up in a comfy chair in front of the fire, always with a book in her hands.

She is a passionate volunteer and supporter of several hearing loss charities, in particular Hearing Dogs for Deaf People and Hearing Link. Living with hearing loss all her life, she is now incredibly lucky to be partnered with her very own Hearing Dog, Lucy.

Also available on Amazon:

THE CAPTAIN'S HOUSE (THE CAPTAIN TRILOGY Book 1)
THE CAPTAIN'S FOLLY (THE CAPTAIN TRILOGY Book 2)

Printed in Great Britain
by Amazon